HOLLOW GIRLS

HOLLOW GIRLS

JESSICA
DRAKE-THOMAS

CEMETERY DANCE PUBLICATIONS

Baltimore

2024

Hollow Girls

Trade Paperback Edition

ISBN:
978-1-58767-972-8

Cemetery Dance Publications
132B Industry Lane, Unit #7
Forest Hill, MD 21050
www.cemeterydance.com

“All things are possible.
Who you are is limited by
who you think you are.”

—*The Egyptian Book of the Dead*

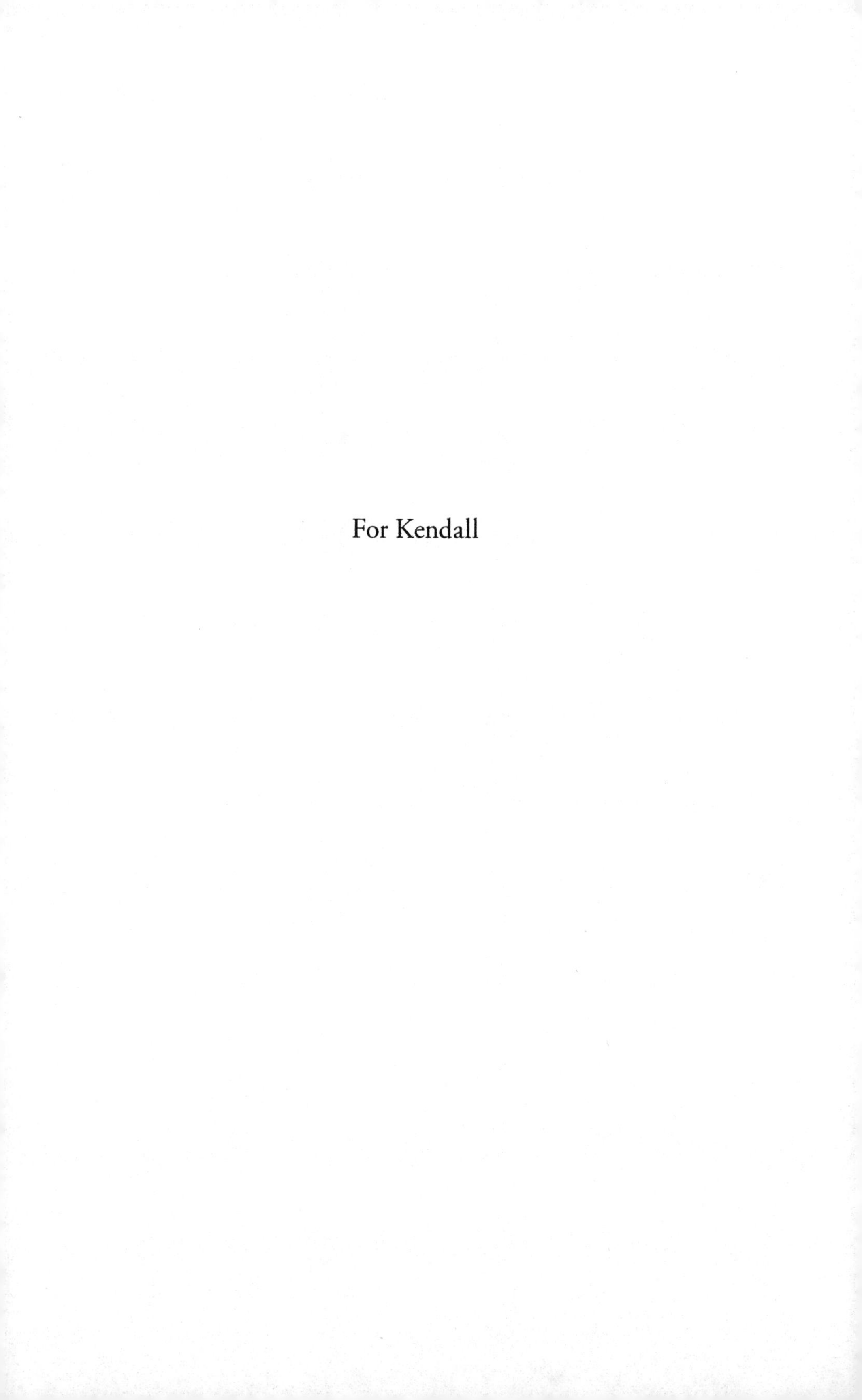

For Kendall

CHAPTER ONE

2024

LATELY, I SEE STACIA EVERYWHERE—on crowded streets, in bars, in the coffeeshop where I get my lunch, even among the visitors at the funeral home where I work. Stacia, with her dark hair and dark eyes, staring right at me and always in my peripheral vision. I can feel the weight of her stare, almost blaming me for walking out of the Deeping Woods alone nearly two decades ago. My pulse races, my palms go sweaty. By the time that I dare to look right at her, Stacia is gone, replaced by a woman who only vaguely looks like her.

This has been happening for two decades. I miss Stacia. She was the only person I've ever met who truly understood me. Although, perhaps, it was because a younger version of me—the girl that I was before I became friends with Stacia—was open to allowing herself be known. I was less frightened then. Less focused on protecting myself from outside influences.

I return home to my apartment. It's in an old building, with softened wood floors and old building smell. It was renovated prior to my moving a few belongings in, but it still has that lived-in, ancient feel. It has gray walls, with black wooden furniture. I have two pictures, in plain frames—one of me and Dad at my college graduation. The other, of me and Stacia, from that fateful summer.

That, and nothing more. After all, I know better than most that human lives are nothing more than waystations. Everyone's just stopping through. Why leave behind a mess for someone else to clean up? Though, I still keep my old protections. Salt, lining the doorways and windows. There are jars, filled with bay leaves and meadow sweet. A few candles. Over the years, I've had a few of the Dead follow me home. I do my best to maintain this space, make my boundaries known.

After securely locking the door, I walk into the tiny kitchenette, my black stilettos clicking on the floor as I pull a bottle of pinot grigio from the fridge. I pour myself a glass as I unbutton my blazer and untuck my white oxford shirt. I close my eyes, letting out a deep sigh I've been holding in. Taking a large gulp of cold, tart wine, I let myself relax.

I've been tense all day. After Mila and I got into an argument, we've been avoiding each other. Hard to do when you work in the same icy morgue. Then, there was a double viewing for a father and his teenage daughter, who had died in a car accident. I couldn't help but think of my own father and how my mother left us when I was the same age as the daughter. I found myself, standing between the two slabs, my eyes on their hands, waxy and pale. My vision blurred with tears. Emotions are an occupational hazard, particularly in the death-care industry. You have to allow them space, or you'll break beneath them.

I'd stepped into my office for a moment alone, before dressing them in their Sunday best for their viewing. I'd sent Dad a text, checking in. I haven't yet gotten a response, though I suppose it's what I should expect, given that we haven't spoken in months. We used to be close. I don't remember exactly when I lost him. He became angry, distracted. Distant. As soon as I got the chance, I left Blackwell, never to return. I feel as though I've been looking for something myself. What that is, I still don't know. Whatever he's looking for, it's in Blackwell. He's never left.

Opening my eyes, I take out my phone. Still, nothing. I slip it back into my blazer pocket, then take another sip of wine. It's so quiet here. It's almost like the quiet has a presence. I'm used to silence. From behind me, in the still-dark depths of the apartment, I hear what sounds like a soft, breathy laugh. I know that laugh, though I've not heard it in years. I freeze, then turn slowly to see what's there.

In the shadows, I see the dark form of a woman, sitting in one of the chairs at my table. My gut knows who it is, though my mind hasn't yet caught up. Stepping forward, I flip the switch, and golden light illuminates the little breakfast nook, revealing my visitor. I gasp, dropping my wine-glass. Far away, I hear it shatter, and cool wine splashes against my ankle. It's drowned out by the sound of my heartbeat, pounding in my ears.

It's been nearly two decades, but I remember Stacia as if I had only saw her yesterday. It's impossible, of course. She went missing twenty-four years ago and I was the last person to see her.

Right now, Stacia's sitting at my table, her legs crossed as she perches on the high-legged chair. It's an older version of her. Something that I never thought that I'd see. Her hair is tumbling over her shoulders. She's dressed in darkness. She wears it like a silk dress, or a velvet cape. I try to wrap my mind around the fact that she's wearing the same clothes that she disappeared in but cannot. There's a dark mist that surrounds her. It makes a low thrumming, as if it has a life and a pulse of its own.

"Where have you been?" I ask. "It's really you, isn't it?"

Stacia smiles. "It's really me. I missed you, Olive." She does not answer the first question.

"How did you get in here?" My landlord is the only person who has keys.

"I traveled through time and space," she says, her eyes turning into two black orbs as her sclera vanishes like paper drenched in ink. "I saw the edges of the world, and I peeled them back like the skin off an orange." The shadows around her darken, the overhead light dimming. Her teeth look longer. Pointier, gray with rot.

I have no idea what I'm supposed to say or do. If I'm being wholly honest, this is the one thing I've been hoping will happen for twenty-four years. Here she is, alive, but something is off. Something that makes my stomach churn.

"I've missed you," I whisper.

Stacia smiles again, the grin splitting her face in two as her lips curl upward. Her skin starts weeping dark liquid from her pores, turning her as black as an oil slick. The only thing that doesn't are her eyes, which become white orbs with tiny points in them. When she opens her mouth, her jaw drops, inhumanly wide. She lets out an awful scream.

I want to scream, but all that comes out is a low moan, which I cover with my hand. I stand there, staring, as Stacia vanishes, leaving me alone again. There's no sign of her—when I move closer to look, there is the merest smudge of what looks like charcoal on the back of the chair. I reach out, my shaky fingers brushing against it. It's slightly damp.

Goosebumps rise, cold on my back, in the space where my neck meets my shoulders. I have this feeling of dread. For the first time in a long time, I really think back to that summer, long ago. It's that space in my memory, the end of the familiar, sane world. *Here, there be monsters.*

My phone rings, and it's like I'm waking from a bad dream to find that I'm home safe. I pull it out of my pocket. The number is withheld. I slide my finger across the screen.

"Hello?"

"May I speak to Olive Sanderson?" His tone is clinical, professional.

"Speaking." My heart does a lolloping thud. He speaks like a police officer.

"This is Detective Bowen from the Blackwell Police Department. I'm sorry to tell you this, but your father's been reported missing."

My hand covers my mouth to muffle the sharp exhalation of air that comes out instead of a scream. It's the two things—first, seeing Stacia, then receiving this news about my father, that makes me certain the two are related.

CHAPTER TWO

1999

IT'S THE SUMMER IN BETWEEN SIXTH and seventh grade when Stacia Kessel and I become best friends. Up until this particular day, all of the girls our age that live in the neighborhood hung out together, a rabble of girls, playing with plastic horses or colorful tulle and polyester dress-up clothing.

This day, Krissy Bradshaw gathers us in her father's garage. It smells of gasoline and cut grass. Neither of Krissy's parents' cars are parked inside. There are smudges of oil marking their respective places. Instead, Krissy's hot pink bicycle is on its side. There are symbols drawn in different colored sidewalk chalk around it.

Krissy is a hellcat dressed in hot pink and jelly shoes, her hair in a scrunchie. Somehow, we end up in a circle, with Stacia standing in the center. She's standing with her hands at her sides. She raises an eyebrow. She's so cool about all of this. As if she's known it was going to happen.

"I'm not crazy about you, Stacia," Krissy says, wrinkling her nose. "Neither is Andi."

All the other girls stand around Stacia in a circle. It's like the Salem Witch Trials, which I'd done a project on for school the year before. Stacia is, undeniably, the only one of us who ever challenged Krissy's eminent domain. She's smarter than Krissy, more creative. Not to mention, she's prettier than Krissy. Any one of these things could have been the reason for Krissy's sudden display of power.

"I don't like you, and neither does Andi or Marissa," Krissy goes on, her hands on her bony hips as she stands confidently.

"Do you?" Krissy asks the next girl, who's wide-eyed. It's like a ritual, each girl proclaiming herself a member of Krissy's inner circle. It's a ruthless move, but Stacia has challenged Krissy's leadership one too many times. As a result, Stacia has to go.

"No." Each girl gives her answer solemnly.

"Do you?" Krissy points with her chin, smiling cruelly.

"No."

I can barely believe what I'm hearing. Everyone's just falling into line. My heart beats nervously, my stomach twisting itself in knots. I know this is wrong. There's an awful allure to the idea of siding with the others. When Krissy reaches me, I can't even answer. I don't want to lose my friends. Don't want to join Stacia in the middle, either. My throat feels tight, and my face is hot with shame.

"Do you, Olive?" Krissy asks, again.

Stacia looks at me, neither hope nor hatred in her stare. Just an overwhelming sense of nonplus. I shrug, watching as Stacia shrugs, too. A small smile has come to Stacia's lips, as if she knows I'm gathering my courage.

Krissy's crossing her arms and tapping her tiny foot. She smells a rat. "Well? Do you?" I shrug again, with one arm. When I glance at Stacia, she's smiling. I'm return Stacia's grin. We're both about to walk through the fire together.

"I don't see why we're doing this. It's stupid, Krissy," I mumble. I'm still mad at Krissy, who invited me over to her house the week before, a seldom occurrence. A chance to be alone with the leader of the group. However, Krissy ordered me to make a trail of red X's in marker on her basement floor. Then, she had gone right to her mother and told.

My own mother was quick to anger. When Krissy's mother had called, I hadn't been able to lie. "Yes, I did it. But she told me to." It had been a lesson in thinking for myself. My trust in Krissy had been broken that day. There was also the time that Krissy had pulled the head off my favorite doll, in retribution for being the center of attention at my own birthday party.

Not getting an answer from me, Krissy sighs, turning to Stacia. "We don't like you. That's all. Maybe you should find new friends."

"Whatever," Stacia drawls. "You don't have to like me." Tearless, she walks from the garage, out into the sweltering sparkle of the summer afternoon. She looks like a cooler version of Princess Leia, in her purple, tie-dye t-shirt and denim cutoffs.

This is the moment that my new self is born, watching as Stacia walks out of that garage, shouldering her way through the circle of girls. I glare at Krissy.

"This was stupid," I say. Then, I turn and follow Stacia out of the garage, leaving the scene of failed carnage behind me.

"Olive?" Krissy demands. "Where are you going? You're choosing her?"

I glance back. They're all still standing in their circle like a bunch of Puritans. In a moment I'll later pride myself on, I nod. "Yeah." Then, I run to catch up with Stacia, who turns to me, and smiles.

"Hey, Olive."

"Hey." I'm a little breathless from running to catch up.

"Thanks for not joining them back there," Stacia says as I slip into step beside her.

"You were brave. I would have cried." I'm really impressed. In this moment, I want to be just like Stacia, to learn her ways.

"That's what they wanted," Stacia says with a bitter laugh.

"True. Still, you were badass." The word in my mouth feels weird, like it's coming from someone else. I stumble over it a little bit, hoping that someday, it'll come out smoother. Cooler.

Stacia beams. "I was, wasn't I?"

"You were." Now, we're friends in a way that we weren't before. We're a united front.

"Want to go and explore the woods?" Stacia asks.

"Sure." Blackwell is a suburb, mostly houses, which sprawls alongside the Deeping Woods. There are legends about children getting lost in the woods, which are at the foot of the Great Smoky mountains.

Stacia and I know that the woods are forbidden. Our parents all tell us not to go too far in, not to leave the paths. There's a sense of fear when they talk about the woods, that we would not return after going in.

We both go and get our bikes, meeting up on the sidewalk, then ride down the street. We ride along the path that cuts through the woods. We sing songs that we've heard on the radio. As it turns out, Stacia, like my dad, listens to Metallica. We both know all the words.

"Perhaps we'll find Jackie Morton," Stacia says, sniffing.

"Maybe." Jackie Morton went missing almost a year before. She had been camping with her parents at one of the campgrounds. Her mother turned away to look up at a large black bird flying overhead. When Mrs. Morton glanced down to say something to Jackie, she was gone. She was twelve years old—our age. She went to the church school on the other side of town, though.

"Some people say that the fairies took her," Stacia says.

"Really? I heard it was a UFO," I murmur, looking at the way the blacktop shimmers in the heat.

"I think they're both the same thing, only going by different names."

Despite how things ultimately end with Stacia's disappearance, I would never sacrifice the time I did have with Stacia for all the popularity in the world. Instead, I become a wild Fae. A witch-child. Even after Stacia disappears, I carry the same mystique, wrapped around me like a second skin. I am the girl who knows too many secrets. Everyone in my small town eventually avoids me like I carry a plague.

CHAPTER THREE

2024

AS SOON AS I ARRIVE IN BLACKWELL, I pull my ancient black Cadillac into the parking lot at the police station. I'm shown into Detective Bowen's office. He shakes my hand— his palm is callused, work-hardened. He has a bit of a paunch forming beneath his tucked-in oxford shirt. I know him, I realize. Back when he wore Doc Martens, with long emo bangs and an eyebrow piercing. I'd dropped a book once. He'd picked it up, handing it to me in return for a mumbled thanks. I've forgotten his name entirely.

"You don't remember me, do you, Olive?" he asks. "We went to high school together, though we never really spoke."

"I remember, Johnny Bowen," I reply, the name coming to me like a half-remembered cantrip. "I had already checked out by then." I wandered through the halls of Blackwell High like a ghost. There, but not really.

He gives me a sad look, nods, then gestures to an open door. "Come on in."

I accept his offer of coffee, and sit there, sipping the bitter but sugary sludge. It only adds to the ache in my gut. He gets out a pad of paper, pulls a pen out of his pocket. I'm filled with dread. This feels like an interrogation.

"Have you found any sign of my dad?" I ask, swallowing the painful lump in the back of my throat. I glance over towards the door, which he's left open.

"No," he says, shaking his head. "We have not."

"Have you checked the woods?" Just the thought of the woods gives me an even worse feeling. Bile rises in the back of my throat. The woods are where people go to vanish.

"Why do you say that?"

"My dad goes fishing every weekend, or he used to." I stare at him. He's biting his lip, tapping his pen against the pad. He's nervous as all get-out. "What are you not telling me, Detective?"

"There are decided links between your father's disappearance and Stacia Kessel's."

Keep yourself composed, Olive. When I think, it's in Stacia's voice. This is oddly calming. I'm a mortician, very talented at compartmentalization, so I give him my most clinical look.

"I'm not wholly surprised, to be honest. This is Blackwell, after all. What have you found?"

To his credit, Detective Bowen maintains eye contact. "There are... things in your father's house—Stacia's missing persons fliers. A notebook. Maps of the Deeping Woods. It looks like he was doing an investigation."

This is a surprise. "Really? Can I see them?" I blurt out.

Detective Bowen shakes his head. "This is an ongoing investigation. It's all in evidence."

That's a no, then, Stacia says in my head, sounding as disappointed as I feel. The thing is, I know all about police procedure. It's the nature of being a mortician. I've done body pickup from crime scenes, back when I was doing a temp job for the County Coroner's office. I've seen things. Corpses in odd positions. Sickening decomposition.

"When was the last time you heard from your father?" he asks.

"He called me while I was at work," I say, pausing before adding, "It was a few weeks ago. We didn't talk long because I was busy... I'm a mortician."

He nods, squinting thoughtfully. "How did he seem?"

"He asked me if I had heard from Stacia, now that you mention it," I say, trailing off as my mind suddenly kicks into high gear. I'm trying to remember everything he'd said to me. "Just that he had found himself a project. I thought he meant a book."

"What did you tell him?" Johnny Bowen asks me.

I smile, the whole room going blurry as I fight back tears. "I told him that I often see her when I'm walking down the street. She's just ahead of me, but then when she turns around, it's someone else."

"I'm sorry," he says. "It must have been hard losing your best friend like that."

I have to look away, down at the cup in my hands. A traitorous tear slips down my cheek. First my mother left, then my best friend disappeared, now my father's gone, too. No one sticks around for me. "I thought the authorities believed Stacia to be dead." I do not want to talk about the cabin—or the night I was found wandering the woods. My shoes gone; my feet cold, covered in mud. There were small amounts of blood—Stacia's—on my shirt.

"Do you believe Stacia to be dead?" he asks me.

Touché, Stacia says in my head, sounding very impressed. I look into his eyes and see pity there. He's got forehead wrinkles, dark circles under his eyes that weren't there when we graduated from high school fifteen years ago.

"Well, I never saw her die, so it stands to reason she could be alive and well." I shrug as I think of all the people who have gone missing in the Deeping Woods over the years. Of all the people who have gone missing in the woods all across the country, without a trace.

He gives me an odd look. "You're the last person to have seen her."

"Believe me. I know." I was questioned thoroughly, back when she had first disappeared. Then, in the months and years following, I was ostracized by the entire community. "Everyone in Blackwell made sure I didn't forget. I had to leave in order to do that." There's a bitterness in my tone that surprises me.

Perhaps if you hadn't been, then you'd have been here for your dad, Stacia says.

But I couldn't have been, I think. *I needed to get out of Blackwell, or I would have ended up gone, too.*

"Is there anywhere that you can think your father might go? Anyone that he might have gone to see?"

I shake my head, even though I know exactly where he might have gone. I just don't want to go there myself. I want the police to go there and look, with their weapons and SWAT gear, though I couldn't say what for. "Have you checked the woods? Over by Snake Creek?"

"We'll take a look, since you mention it," he says, writing it down on his pad. "Not to worry—there were no signs of foul play at his house. I'm sure that we'll find him, safe and sound."

I nod, but I can't help but hear Stacia, in my mind: *You know that when Those That Live in the Woods want someone, they'll keep them. Forever.*

Detective Bowen's giving me a kind smile. He means well or attempts to. I can tell. But the damage has already been done. My best friend disappeared almost two decades ago without a trace. I have not been in the Deeping Woods since. I hope that I don't have to go back in there to get my dad. If it comes down to it, I might have to. It's the one thing I'm afraid of.

"Thank you, Detective," I say.

"Call me Johnny," he replies, shaking my proffered hand. His grip is firm, his hand warm and sweaty.

"Olive." I'm uncomfortable, so I smile, then turn to go.

"Are you going to be okay?" he asks, causing me to freeze.

I turn, giving him a stern look. "No, but I'm going to try to be."

"Well, you can call me," he offers, holding out a business card. I take it, stuffing it in my pocket, where it will remain, forgotten and unused.

"Search the woods by Snake Creek," I tell him as I turn to go. "That's where he fishes." Because if the police don't check the woods, then I'm going to have to. Though, I trusted the police once before, and they failed. I think of all those who have gone missing in the Deeping Woods. I don't want to add my father to that list. Not yet.

After all, I came back. Though, for the life of me, I don't remember how. There's a blank space in my memory, one which hangs heavy like storm clouds.

HOLLOW GIRLS

Two girls go into the woods. Only one returns. The other girl is never seen or heard from again. The woods swallow her up whole. You'd think there was some sort of lesson in this. In all the fairy tales, there's a reason why—the girl who survives is morally pure. Perfect, in every way. But I'm not good at all—I'm fallible, broken.

Stacia was the girl who went into the forest, never to return. I was the one who survived.

For the life of me, I don't know why.

CHAPTER FOUR

2000

THE DAY MY MOTHER LEAVES US IS A day like any other. Stacia and I spend the day in the woods, prowling about. We are still searching for Jackie. In the time we've been looking, there have been two more disappearances. We have pictures, which we take on a disposable camera. Shoe prints. Deflated mylar balloons. Plastic bags.

"Look at this," Stacia says, pausing. I move closer, to stand beside her. It's a perfect ring of toadstools on the forest floor. The dark soil they grow in is lush, black. I sniff, smelling something rotting.

"A fairy ring?" I ask. We are voracious readers of myths and fairy stories. We devour them like wolves, eager for more. The local library can barely keep up with us. We're always requesting more.

"What if all of the disappearances in these woods are because of the Fae?" Stacia muses, ratcheting the turn wheel on the camera, then snapping another picture.

"Then we're going about this all wrong," I say, immediately catching on. "We've been looking for a human reason...or animal."

"You're right," Stacia agrees. We smile at each other, our minds already coming up with known Fae traps: iron, milk, bread, cake.

Stacia and I part ways in the middle of Banks Street, in front of my parents' house. I don't notice anything's different. Everything seems the same, until I walk into the living room and find my father sitting on the couch in tears.

"Dad?" My voice is small. I'm shaken to my very foundations because never have I seen my big bear of a father cry before. As I look around, nothing is missing or broken—my mother's trinkets, the pictures of her side of the family, those awful doe-eyed Precious Moments figurines she loves are all still here.

Dad gestures for me to come over. So, I sit down beside him on the couch, and he wraps one of his big bear arms around me. He smells of sweat and laundry detergent.

"It's your mother." His voice breaks on *mother*.

White hot fear shoots through me, blanking out my thoughts. "She's dead?"

"No. She's—she's left us."

"Is she coming back?" I'm confused. After all, my mother has often gone away without us, many times before. She would always meet up with her sorority sisters to go on fancy beach vacations to places with names that sounded like brands of fruity drinks or salsa.

My father sniffles, taking in deep breaths. "No. Not this time, sweetheart. She's—she's left you a note, to explain." He sniffles again, reaching for the envelope on the coffee table. It's flecked with tears—my father's, I realize. I feel nothing but tenderness towards him. Then fear, because what if he wants to leave, too? Then what will I do?

I take the envelope, setting it down beside me. Dad uses one of his big hands to wipe at his face, ending by tugging on his gingery beard. His other arm stays wrapped around my thin shoulders.

"Are—are you okay?" I ask, wondering how I'm supposed to convince him to stay.

"No. No, but I suppose I will be. It's just us now, Olive."

"You're not going anywhere, are you?" Fear of finding myself all alone is a dark shadow, slinking out of the woods to swallow me whole.

Dad blinks, his eyes watery with tears. He pulls me even closer, so my head ends up lodged between his shoulder and his chin. "No," he promises me, speaking into the top of my head. "I'm not going anywhere."

"Good. I'm not either," I whisper, my throat tight with emotion.

He kisses me on the hair. His tears drip down on my part. He sobs, a heartrending sound, then lets me go. He wipes at his face. Sniffling, he looks at me. "Are you hungry? Can you eat?"

"Yeah, Dad," I say. He pats me on the back, then gets up, going into the kitchen. He's still crying, softly. I stay on the couch, looking at the envelope. I can hear Dad in the kitchen, opening the spice cabinet, then the refrigerator.

Dad doesn't know how to cook, I think, my love for him a glowing ember in the center of my chest. He would never abandon me. Not of his own accord. That's what I learn this day when he becomes my only family.

I take the envelope upstairs to my room, where I stuff it into the top drawer of my desk. I have no desire to read whatever apology Mom wrote. She has abandoned us, plain and simple. Part of me wants to scream. The other part wants to break down into tears. I do love her, and I can't believe she's just gone. A third part of me knows that someone has to keep it together— for Dad.

Despite the sharp pain in my chest, I walk over to my overstuffed bookshelves, where I slip out the kid's cookbook that I'd gotten a few Christmases ago, then brought it downstairs to the kitchen, where Dad has taken out a box of pasta. When he sees what I've brought him, his face crumples, as if he's going to cry again.

"They're easy," I assure him, opening it up, to the recipe for meat sauce. He places a hand on my shoulder, then ruffles my hair.

"Thank you, Olive," he whispers.

"I think we have ground beef in the fridge," I inform him, matter-of-factly. We are going to survive. If Mom doesn't need us, then we don't need her either. I will always worry whether or not I'm good enough. I will doubt myself, going into any new situation. But the one person who I know will never vanish without telling me is my father. He's been in and out of touch, but he's steady, constant. That's why, when he goes missing, I know he didn't go of his own accord.

CHAPTER FIVE

2024

I LEAVE THE POLICE STATION, THEN GO and sit out in my car. The air is hot, and I grip the steering wheel, letting the heat sear my palms, my lungs. A thin layer of sweat rises across my upper lip. I let out a deep breath of hot air as think back to the day that my mother left. She had been planning it, for a long time. She hadn't just woken up and decided to go.

I don't remember much of my mother. Her bright clothing. Her pale pink lipstick, which reminded me of cupcake frosting. Her orangey fake tan, her bottle blonde hair, the red roots showing when she was late to the salon. The romance novels that lay scattered in her wake.

Though my father and I have drifted apart, my worry for him is a hard stone in the pit of my stomach. I've learned how to keep going forward, even though all my senses are telling me to stop. The clinical approach to something upsetting. Like making a scalpel incision, shoulder to sternum, shoulder to sternum, then down to the navel, opening them up. The first time I did it, I was terrified that the corpse's eyes would animate, blood would spill out the slice like syrup, that she'd start screaming. She did not.

My phone rings, NUMBER WITHHELD. As I watch, the letters turn into numbers and then strange symbols. Fragmenting into pixels. Unreality washes over me. I answer, half-expecting it to be the police calling. "Hello?"

There's a crackle. "Olive?" It's Stacia. She sounds as though she's speaking from a long distance. Perhaps, through time and space. I feel like the bottom has just fallen out of the world. Like the ground has flipped, and now I'm falling upward and into the sky.

"Stacia? Where are you?" I'm gripping the phone in one hand, the steering wheel in the other. Despite the heat, I'm cold all over.

"You *know* where." There's a scream, and Stacia yells, *Olive*, another burst of static comes, then the line goes dead. A memory surfaces—Stacia, holding a flashlight, turning towards me in the dark, her eyes wide in fear. *Olive*, she mouths. *Help me.* Something moves in the shadows behind her. Context is on the other side of the dark door in my mind, this is the first memory I've had of that night in years.

Unnerved, hands shaking, I set the phone down on the passenger seat beside my purse. *I must go home*, I think. Putting the key into the ignition, I drive through the familiar streets of Blackwell. Inherently, I know the place has changed. It's not as shiny as it once was. It's got the feel of a place that's been lived in for a while. Not much is new. Still the same houses, though there are small changes. There's a Starbucks now. The diner and the IGA look faded.

When I pull up in front of my father's house, I feel like I'm being broken open. It's a two-story, white craftsman, with green shutters and a door to match. The Japanese maple still stands out front, along with the fake wishing well. His ancient, white Ford truck still sits in the driveway, paint flaking off.

I let myself inside, the deadbolt turning over with a familiar click. Stepping inside, I stand by the door, expecting Dad to come and greet me. It's a punch to the gut when I'm met by silence.

It smells the same as it has since my mother left—lemon Pinesol, laundry detergent, and Folger's coffee. Mom had more expensive tastes. She took them with her when she left. I glance around at the familiar and worn plaid sofa, the dark mahogany furniture. There's a layer of dust over everything.

Some people belong to a place. It's in their blood, their bones. That's how my dad belongs to Blackwell, this house. They're made of the same stuff—dark dirt and small-town secrets. I move through the house like a ghost, looking for something out of place. Seeing nothing, I make my way to the kitchen. I kick off my shoes.

I leave my purse on the kitchen table, then take the stairs down to the basement. My father has a woodworking shop down there. At the bottom, my bare feet touch the cold concrete floor. The darkness smells of concrete, wood shavings, polyurethane. I reach up, pulling the knotted string on the single lightbulb. It clicks on, throwing dim light over the familiar sight of wood, saws, and other machinery.

Dad is a local historian, an avid researcher, delving into local lore. No doubt, whatever he found was related to the Deeping Woods. In fact, I know it in my gut. He went searching for it. From personal experience, I know the woods are not what they seem. It could be anything.

His saws have been pushed to the walls. His tools are in neat, organized rows on the shelves. The worktable is completely cleared of whatever was on it. I'm sure the police have found whatever Dad thought wasn't valuable to his research.

I smile to myself. The police don't know about the false wall my father put in, behind the shelves to the left. I step over, throwing the hidden switch that causes the shelves to swing outward towards me, revealing the other room. One he made in the event we needed to hide. His panic room, I guess.

Reaching inside, I pull the string to illuminate the tiny space. I'm not surprised to find dad's research into Stacia's disappearance is a lot more detailed than the police even knew. The wall farthest away from me is covered in newspaper clippings and a map of Deeping Woods.

On it, there are marked where disappearances occurred. The caves running underneath Blackwell and the woods are marked out. Different entryways into the systems, too. I look it over. The disappearances are linked—each pin is near to an entrance to the caves. I check the dates—some of them are recent. The oldest date is 1810. *Viola P.* No last name, age seven. All of them are girls, I note. All children.

The tiny foldout table has several notebooks piled on top of it. I begin to look through them, an uncomfortable feeling spreading throughout my stomach. With utter certainty, I know that my father has gone into the woods. I have a sickening feeling he has gone in search of whoever made these girls vanish.

Over a span of two hundred years.

I wonder if he's gone in search of whatever it was Stacia and I found all those years ago. Remembering what I saw in the car—Stacia, standing in the dark—we didn't just go into the woods, we went into the caves.

I turn a notebook page to find an article, the paper yellowed, taped to the page beneath: *Local Girl Missing, Friend Discovered Wandering Woods Alone.* My vision blurs as tears fill my eyes. I remember shivering as I walked, my bare feet stinging with cold as the mud made sucking sounds with each step. I had been bone tired. I couldn't remember who I was, why I was there, or even how long I had been walking.

Something bad happened that night. Something so bad that my mind blocked it out. My stomach does another queasy flip. Two girls go into the caves: only one comes out. Whatever happened, whatever I saw, I was never the same again.

CHAPTER SIX

2000

I SEE MY MOTHER EVERY TIME I LOOK IN the mirror. The contours of her face there but softened in my own. I lean in, towards the glass. "I wish I couldn't see her," I whisper, the weight of her betrayal weighing upon me.

For a brief moment, the summer sun is turned dark, and I see something else in the mirror: a horrible thing in a mask that's been pieced together from skin with ragged stitches. Two black, oily eyes peer out from the holes. Thick hanks of straw are sewn about the head. It's painted red, no...covered in blood.

Reaching up with shaking hands, I feel the flayed material, soft, damp, as it slides over my skin. My hands, too, have been slipped into this skin, the seams lined in thick black thread. When I press the skin, blood oozes out from the stitches, rolling down my cheek like a tear. Opening my mouth, I bare my spiny teeth. This isn't me. It cannot be.

A dark female shadow steps out from behind me. Her hair is matted. She makes a clicking noise, as her dark, knobby hand rests upon my shoulder. She has long, dirty nails. Frozen in fear, there's nothing I can do. She has been hiding behind me all along: my shadow self. She's coming for me. I awake with a gasp to find myself safe in my bed. My pulse races. I've been having this dream ever since my mother left us, two months ago.

When I come downstairs, the kitchen smells of coffee and toast—familiar, comforting smells. Dad looks up from the paper. He's dressed for work, in his button-up shirt and soft sweater. It's always ice cold inside the Historical Society. He's wearing his usual navy khakis.

"You going out with Stacia?" he asks.

"Yup." I'm relieved he never asks where we're going. We always go into the woods, despite constant warnings not to. Children, particularly girls, have gone missing there.

"Be careful," he says. "With that little girl that's gone missing and all."

"I will, Dad." I take a bite of toast, eating it standing by the counter. There's that unspoken agreement I must come home, or else he'll be wrecked.

"I'll be with Stacia the whole time, I promise," I say around a mouthful of toast with honey.

He nods, rustling his paper as he reads it. "I'll be at work until seven tonight. There's that fundraiser gala thing." His work is inconsistent with his appearance. He's a heavy-set man, yet he moves silently through the stacks of documents, newspapers, and other Blackwell memorabilia.

"OK." My bad dream clings to me like oil, black and iridescent.

"Olive?" He's studying me closely—like I'm a historical document, albeit a newer one. One in a language he doesn't fully understand.

"Yes?"

"Where do you girls go?"

"Out," I say, shrugging my shoulder. "We kinda wander around Blackwood." I raise my eyes to meet his. He knows, I realize. He knows everything.

"Just promise me something," he says.

"What?" I ask, my mouth going dry.

"Come back home, Olive. I—" he pauses, sadly. He doesn't finish the sentence. My stomach drops, and I nod.

"Of course, Dad. I promise."

"Thank you," he says. Years later, I will wonder if this is the reason why I survived.

Quickly, I finish my toast, washing it down with a swig of orange juice. I wave to Dad, then run out of the house where Stacia's waiting for me on the sidewalk. Already, the sun is beating down on the blacktop, making waves in the air.

"We'll head out and into the woods," Stacia is saying as we walk to the convenience store down the street. "There has to be somewhere they haven't looked for Jackie Morton."

"Yeah." In my mind, I've been worrying about the feeling of loss I've been experiencing. I keep going over my last interactions with my mother—how did I miss the final goodbye in her eyes? I can't tell this to Stacia. Not yet.

"Are you alright?" she asks. "You're very quiet." I glance over at her. It's like she can read my mind. Years later, I am positive this is why she was taken—because she has some sort of ability to do a deeper read on the universe. A sensitivity other people don't have.

"I'm just… sad, I guess." I don't want to talk about my nightmare. I still feel as though I've somehow lost myself. Mourning that deep feeling of loss.

"About your mom?" she asks. I can't look at her, or I think I'll cry. I keep my eyes on the sidewalk, which is shot through with cracks.

"Yeah." It's true.

"It's okay to be sad, you know?"

I nod, swallowing the lump in my throat as I look at the scuffed toes of my Converse. She nudges me with her bony elbow. "Owww," I say. When I look over at her, she's smiling at me. "Watch out, Toothpick!"

"Come on," she says, opening the glass door to the convenience store. "Snacks are on me today." It smells of slushies in here. It's cold and clean, filled with the hum of the refrigerators.

Together, we both fill up a basket with candy bars, Gatorade, and pre-made sandwiches. Necessary for long wandering treks through the woods, in search of missing children or signs of the Fae. According to our reading, the Fae like sweets. So, we add individually wrapped Twinkies and a carton of milk to our loot.

When we arrive at the register, Harley "Horrorshow" McCallis and Johnny Bowen are standing there, cans of Orange Crush in their hands.

"Look Johnny! It's Olive and Stacia, the town lesbos," Harley says. He got his nickname from his obsession with horror movies. He's always wearing a black t-shirt, emblazoned with the movie poster from *Halloween, Nightmare on Elm Street,* or *Hellraiser.*

"Lesbos is an island, asshole," Stacia snaps as we set our loot on the counter for Harley's teenaged brother to ring up. It's almost as though we're not really there. I feel my face heating up. It's as if Harley can see into me—into the darkest place, where I'm honest with myself. *Am I*? I wonder. *Maybe*, an unfamiliar voice replies. *Why are you attracted to men, too?* Growing up in the early 2000's in a small town in Kentucky, I don't have the language to describe myself.

"What do you do out there, in the woods?" Johnny Bowen asks us.

"We look for the lost children," I say.

"No one's ever found them," Horrorshow says. "It's some old pedo. Or a doomsday cult. Or the ghost of Old Witch Annabelle." He speaks with a high level of jadedness for someone who spends their time watching fake blood spurt across the TV screen.

"We might. We'll let you know when we do," I mutter. Old Witch Annabelle is a local urban legend. Apparently, she killed her daughter on Halloween. She was hanged for it, and ever since, her ghost has wandered the woods.

"That'll be the day," Horrorshow says, rolling his eyes. His eyes stop mid-roll, widening as an idea comes to him. "Maybe you'll be taken, too."

"Or maybe *you'll* be taken, Harley," Stacia says, turning to me. "*Unawares*," she mouths. I cover my mouth to keep from laughing.

"That will be ten forty," the cashier says in a bored, fed-up tone. He throws a glance over at Harley and Johnny. "And then you two are going to pay the two fifty you owe for those cokes." South of the Mason Dixon, every soda's a coke.

"Leo!" Horrorshow groans to his older brother. "What about your employee discount?"

Stacia pays, then we give both boys withering looks before we take our plastic bag of food and leave, the hot summer air enveloping us in a massive blast as we leave the air conditioning of the store.

"Horrorshow's had it out for me since the picture I drew of him as a pig on a motorcycle won the school art show," Stacia mutters. We both glance at each other and giggle. That was classic Stacia. She always fights back, but in a smart way. One where she won't get caught.

"We've got our stuff," I say, reaching into the bag and pulling out a Twix bar. I tear open the wrapper and take a bite of cookie and caramel, covered by chocolate. The best thing about Twix is that you get two.

"Yeah, we do," Stacia says around a bite of her own candy bar. "Let's go to the woods." The woods are where we go to be alone. None of the other children go out there since it's been deemed unsafe. Only grown men go there, to fish in the Snake River that runs through the center.

We leave the path soon after it plunges into the woods. Stacia has a compass, which is on a lanyard around her neck. We've been wandering through these parts for a few years now. We know where we're going.

"Let's go this way," Stacia suggests. We walk along the creek, our shoes sinking a little into the soft mud. "Have you noticed how all of the people who have gone missing are children?"

"Yeah. All girls," I add. "Maybe Horrorshow is right. Maybe it is some sort of a pedo." I don't like admitting it, but it's something that has to be said—we do have to consider this is someone who can overpower two girls.

"We should really have a weapon," Stacia says.

"What kind of a weapon?" I'm thinking along the lines of a gun. Though, the potential for disaster makes me uneasy. My skin prickles with an icy, nameless fear. I look over at the creek, where I see something long and dark slither beneath the water. Kelpie, I think—the dark horse creature which stole children stupid enough to ride its back into the Unseelie Court. All around me is darkened, like a cloud passing over the sun.

"A knife." Stacia speaks so confidently, drawing me suddenly out of the nightmare world. It's like she's already got one in mind. I look at her, blinking in the sunlight.

"Do you have one?"

"My Dad has a hunting knife he doesn't use," she replies. "I think we can borrow it."

"Okay," I say, my mind on other things. Dad has been crying, late at night, when I've been pretending to sleep. He drinks one too many beers and it leaves him maudlin. I look up into the emerald green of the leaves. Sun filters through them, and birds are flitting from branch to branch.

I love walking along the creek, looking into the cold, clear water to find tadpoles or the little black fish that swim there. Sometimes, we find garter snakes. We find no signs of other people out this way. There are no wrappers or other trash, like we find around the park. People don't come out this far into the woods. I've never seen anything out of the ordinary. Until today.

"Look!" Stacia says, pulling me out of my thoughts. When I look, she's pointing, her face solemn. There's a little, moss-covered stone path through the woods. It's just visible through the underbrush.

"Where do you think it goes?"

"To the Black Well," Stacia says with surprising confidence. When I frown at her, she explains, "The one that our town gets its name from."

"Where did you hear that?" I've heard it, from my father. He's a town historian, though. He says the well no longer exists— that it may never have existed to begin with. It's more of a legend than anything else.

Stacia shrugs. "I—I don't know," she says, matter-of-factly. "I just—heard it in my head."

When she says it, I get a cold shock. I raise an eyebrow. I should be used to things like this. Stacia's got one finger on the pulse of things. She knows all about something, just by looking at it. Almost as if the world whispers its secrets to her. Meanwhile, I sense nothing. It's like my senses are dulled—like maybe I'm rolled up in bubble wrap. Suddenly, I wish that I was, if only a little, tuned into the vibrations of things, too. But I'm not.

"What else did you hear?" I ask curiously.

"Bad things happened at the Black Well," she goes on, her dark eyes wide with gravity. "Dark things, which left a permanent stain on the land."

My knees lock, because this phrasing is exactly the same as Dad used, when he was reading it from a document hundreds of years old. I can recall the paper was yellow and crumbling with age. The writing was spidery.

Stacia continues a few steps before stopping and turning towards me. She tilts her head to the side, smiling. "It's alright, Olive. They can't hurt us." She holds out her hand. I nod, then take Stacia's hand. I don't believe in ghosts. But I believe in Stacia. We go down the path, where the old stones are slick.

At the end of the stone path, there's a clearing. It's grown wild, sunlight filtering in through the leaves overhead. From where we stand, we can see a cabin. At one time, it was painted green, but it's mostly flaked away, leaving raw, grayed wood behind. The roof is moss-covered, there's a bit of charring at the windows.

Wind blows through the leaves, stirring the underbrush. All around us, it sounds like the woods are whispering. My skin rises in goosebumps. There's an odd pressure, in between my shoulder blades, as if Stacia and I are being watched. I twirl around, finding nothing.

"Do you hear that? That whispering?" Stacia asks.

"Yes." Even I can hear it, which makes things worse. I can't ever hear anything. I can almost make out the words. It's like a language that I once knew but have since forgotten.

"It feels like we're not alone." Stacia sounds nervous, which makes me freeze up. Then Stacia laughs, throwing her head back. I feel a rush of relief. There's a part of this only she can hear. Whatever it is, Stacia's not afraid of it. Wanting to be a part of the game, I laugh too. Stacia grabs both of my hands, then we begin to spin in circles.

The sun seems brighter suddenly. The world spins as I raise my face towards the sun. Stacia lets go of my hands, and we both look up. All around us, there's the soft whispering of the wind in the leaves. My dizzy head swims. We're both breathing heavily. Stacia sighs.

"Let's go see what's inside," she says. I nod, then follow her.

Inside of the cabin, there's a jumble of things. Old, decaying furniture. A cloudy, cracked mirror hangs upon the wall. Papers, which have been rained on, the words a blur. There's charring on the walls, and around the fireplace. I look up, to find the roof is mostly there. Here and there, holes are in the ceiling. But with the way the woods have grown around it, the place is protected. It's still a safe place.

"I wonder who lived here," I say, reaching up to wipe some of the grime off the mirror. My own eye peers back through the clear space in the accumulated grit. I think briefly of something I've read: mirrors as portals to another world.

"Someone special," Stacia tells me. "Someone… like us." That makes me feel better—Stacia's always doing that. Always including me, even though she's the one who's special.

Stacia sits down on one of the chairs. I sit in the other. The tabletop is weathered, with dry leaves scattered across its surface. I tug at a splinter which is coming free.

"This is spooky," I say, glancing around. I've got the overwhelming feeling we're trespassing. There are animal skulls, lining the mantel over the hearth.

"Very. Let's have this be our clubhouse," Stacia suggests. "We can use it as a base camp for our searches."

I'm uneasy; there's still a lingering feeling that we're in someone else's home. Despite the knowledge no one's been here in a long while, I feel as though that person might come back at any time to find us trespassing. "Are you sure?"

"Yes. It feels good here. We can bring a tarp to fix the roof, and then we can bring books and some other things to keep here."

"What if someone else finds it?" I wonder aloud.

"Olive, no one else comes out here," Stacia says. "It's just us. Anyway, we can put a lock on the door."

I bite the insides of my cheeks. That's true enough. All the other kids prefer to be in town. The boys all hang out at the arcade, and the girls our age hang out at Krissy's. Me and Stacia, the town's outsiders at twelve, hang out in the woods. Exactly where our parents tell us not to go.

"Well?" Stacia arches her eyebrow. We won't do it if I say no, but I can tell that she really wants this. I can't deny her anything.

"Let's do it." We beam at each other. Finally, a place for us. We have nowhere in town we can go without being ridiculed. No one believes we're going to find Jackie. Especially since the police have failed. That was why we go into the woods. It's our safe haven, and now, it's given us a place to call our own.

We clear off a spot on the table where we create a small altar to the Fae. I open the carton of milk and set it down beside an unwrapped Twinkie.

"To all the Fae," Stacia says. "Hear us and come commune. We thank you for sending us a space. We want to share it with you." These lines are directly from Rowena Pennyworth's book, *Dealings with the Fae*. We've read it so often, the words tumble out in perfect unison, sounding exactly like an incantation.

"We come in peace," I add. "We mean you no harm."

"Partake of our offering," Stacia finishes. We're both silent for a moment, listening to the sound of the wind in the trees, deep like a heartbeat. I feel a pressure, between my shoulders, like I'm being watched.

"Let's head home," I say. Together, we pack up our things. As we walk away, we hear something moving through the brush. It sounds like it's running. When we turn back, we see nothing. Our gazes meet. My heart is racing.

"Come on," Stacia says, smiling knowingly as she tugs on my arm. "Let's go, Olive."

CHAPTER SEVEN

2024

I'M STANDING JUST OUTSIDE OF MY father's bedroom. The door is closed. Reaching up, I place my palm flat against the cold, white-painted wood. Wild grief passes through me, lancing like a knife. Nothing stirs within the room. It's empty.

Even so, I place my other hand on the knob, turning it. Pushing the door inward, I peer inside to find it exactly as Dad left it. In the darkness, I see his rumpled bed. Books are piled on his nightstand. A glass of water, half-drunk. The closet door is ajar, his sweaters hanging like withered, starving animals.

Nothing is amiss here. I'm looking for clues and seeing none. That's the problem. That lack of anything. It's been so long since I've been here, that I wouldn't even know if anything were out of place.

Going around Dad's house, I make sure that all the doors and windows in the house are locked. It's weird because I've never had to do this at this house before. He's always been here, to make sure it was safe.

I have the odd, lurking sensation that I'm being watched. A soft prickle, between my shoulders at the nape of my neck. I peer out the window over the back door. It's dark out. I stand there, staring. There are bushes in the back yard. Behind them, there's another yard and a house. No lights are coming through the windows.

I shake off the feeling. Sometimes, I feel this way. Not to this extreme, however. I check the deadbolt is in place. It is. I even go so far as to pull the blinds and the chain.

As I check the windows, I'm thinking about that cabin, something I haven't thought about in ages. I know everything started that day and ended with the night Stacia vanished.

Once finished, I grab my bag, which I've left by the door. I go upstairs to my bedroom, hauling my duffle over my shoulder. The steps creak familiarly, the old wood protesting beneath my feet. I'm exhausted. Years have passed, and nothing has changed up here—the walls are still lilac-colored. Everything is where I left it.

The My Chemical Romance posters, my old necklaces and bracelets, the books on the Fae that I haven't touched in so long—there's a light coating of dust over them. Spell materials are still in their bottles and jars. My old paperbacks, their spines broken and peeling.

Except the top drawer to my dresser is open, like a drooping jaw. When I look in, I notice immediately the letter from my mother is gone. It was the only thing left, after all my clothes were emptied from the drawers when I left for college. I frown. Why would Dad want that? How did he even know it was there?

Suddenly, I wish just once, I had been curious about that letter. That I had at least read it one time. But I hadn't. In the months leading up to my mother leaving, we had fought. She had wanted me to take more of an interest in church.

I didn't. Like my father, I was a card-carrying heathen. The two of us would stay home on Sundays, while she went alone. We would watch cartoons and read the funnies. Did he try to get in touch with Mom, after all these years? He might have, though I can't for the life of me, figure out why.

She left, and then never tried to get in touch. She abandoned us. Maybe Dad was looking for some sort of closure. Closure is something I understand.

I go back downstairs to the kitchen. When I open the refrigerator, I can smell that something's gone bad. I grab one of Dad's beers. I twist off the cap and take a swig. Drop the cap on the counter with a clink.

The glass bottle is cold and wet with condensation. The beer is nearly flavorless.

When I turn back to the table, I notice the paper is out on the table where Dad left it before he walked out on his life. Sitting down, I open it up. It's dated several days ago— August 5th. The front page has a school picture of a doe-eyed young girl.

Apparently, Dad is not the only one to have gone missing. A young girl, aged five. Another child, lost in the woods. No trace of her. Another, familiar cold prickle waves over my skin. Something is out there. Something that sleeps for years and then wakes up to take small children, and sometimes, older ones.

It has to be a person, though. Right? A person has taken the children. They would be old now, but surely that's what's going on? Two hundred years, though.

Tucking my long hair behind my ears, I go to the obituaries, while I think. As a mortician, it's a professional habit. Usually, I'm the one to help the family place the obits. I'm surprised to find a familiar face, smiling back at me. Hope Bradbury. It's a picture from when I knew her—back when I was in the eighth grade. The year of Stacia's disappearance.

During the darkest time in my life, Miss Bradbury was there, cheering me on. Her memorial service is tomorrow. I owe it to her to show up. And maybe, I can find out if anyone else in town knows what my dad was looking for. I finish my beer, leaving the empty bottle in the sink.

Refolding the paper, I make my way back to my bedroom, turning all the lights out as I go. I want to feel comfort here, being at home. But now that I may have lost my one remaining parent, everything feels like it has sharp edges. The safety and security I usually feel here has been stripped away.

The air here feels charged with danger. People go into the woods and vanish. Except for me. I can't remember what I did to save myself. If I could, then maybe I can save Dad.

Laying back on my bed, I close my eyes. I exhale. I think of Stacia, backlit by the sun. Dad, reaching out to ruffle my hair. Even Mom, tucking me into this very bed. I can't help but think the word "lost" means so many different things. My exhausted body drifts into a deep sleep.

There's something at the window. I can hear it, tapping with a long-nailed finger. When I turn my face, I can see a dark figure, peering in at me. It's backlit by the streetlights. With the way the light hits it, I can't see its features.

It's nothing more than a shadow, hunched over and peering in at me. Long, dark hair frames its pallid face. I can feel it, looking at me. It knows me. I try to move, but I'm frozen. I can hear the soft sound of a young girl, crying. My heartbeat is loud in my ears.

A chill travels over my skin. As I watch, horrified, the creature's breath spreads across the surface of the glass. The finger, nail dragging across the glass, writes in the fog. It's in a language that I don't understand, but I know I once did.

Using its long, slim fingers, it opens the window. I still cannot move. It puts one long leg into the room, followed by another, and then, another. It creeps in, its elongated face hanging over me.

My eyes fly open, and I sit up in bed, looking around. My heart pounds in my chest— ba-BOOM, ba-BOOM, BA-boom, BA-BOOM. My breathing is fast. I remember the last time I felt like this. I've avoided all situations like this ever since.

As I sit up, I see a dark figure move back from the window. Its spindly fingers curl into a fist as it drops out of sight. Except, in the window, written in the fog from its breath, it says— *Welcome Home, Olive.*

When I run across my room, whoever it was is gone. I look out. There is a two-story drop beneath my window. Nothing to stand on or climb up. Whoever was just looking in my window had to have been floating.

CHAPTER EIGHT

2024

THE ONE MORTUARY IN TOWN HAS been in service for over one hundred years. It's in a yellow Victorian house with white gingerbread trim. It almost seems too cheery to be a funeral home. But it's been in the Boyle family for its entire history. It has always been a funeral home.

It was a calming place for me, growing up. Whenever something bad happened, the whole town came here. For solace in the face of loss. It was here that I decided I wanted to be a mortician, when I saw how Lloyd Boyle helped people. I wanted that, too.

My father was disappointed that I didn't follow him into the town archives. I know he understood why I had to leave. Why I had to forge my own path.

When I enter, it's clear the whole town has shown up for Miss Bradbury. She was the kindest teacher at Blackwell Middle. I stand by the door for a little. Inside, the walls are peach with dark wood paneling. There's a crystal chandelier in front of the sweeping staircase. I recall all the funerals I've attended here over the years.

I wave to Lloyd Boyle, now white-haired. He beams and hands me a memorial card. I glance at it briefly, seeing Miss Bradbury's school picture. On the back, a poem by Tennyson.

"Good to see you, Olive. I'm so sorry about Merrick," Lloyd says.

"Thank you." He squeezes my hand. In a moment, he's off to help someone else. He's going at the same pace I usually do. I tuck the card into my blazer pocket.

I'm not used to being at a funeral and not working. Standing here as a guest is like being in an alternate reality. I'm used to keeping everything moving. I'm in my work clothes, with my black Dooney and Bourke handbag slung over my shoulder. I don't know what to do with myself.

"Olive Sanderson? Is that you?" She's still blonde. Still pretty, though she's dressed in a Lilly Pulitzer ensemble that looks like something that you'd wear to a barbeque. Around her neck is a delicate gold cross on a chain. Red stones, dark as heart's blood, are set into it.

"Yeah." I'm a little shocked, though I suppose I shouldn't be. Her smile is lined in bright pink. I don't think she owns black. A small, blonde girl is being dragged along in her wake. She's clasping her hand tightly. Her eyes are wide, her mouth a grim line. She looks just like her mother did, back when we were that age.

"It's me! Krissy Bradshaw, although now it's Bedecker." So, she married the hot shot lawyer who lives in town. Interesting.

"Wow. You look great," I say. And she does. I know that I've got dark, puffy circles under my eyes. I attempted to cover them, but no makeup is strong enough to cover grief, worry. No perfect flip of the eyeliner can fix what's wrong with me.

"Thanks! I was so sorry to hear about your father," she says, her brow creasing in concern that I don't buy for a second. "Have they found any sign of him?"

"Not yet." I've sucked the insides of my cheeks in, and I'm biting them—a nervous habit that has caused my inner cheeks to have lines of scar tissue. I can taste iron already.

"Well, if you need anything, I only live a few blocks away," Krissy says. "Harlon and I bought the house next door to my parents."

"Thanks. I think I'm okay."

"Oh, honey. Really. It's okay to not be okay." Krissy wrinkles her little button nose. "I'll bring you over a casserole."

"That's so kind. You don't have to." I remember the tribunal that Krissy held for Stacia. Deep down, I know that someone like Krissy can never truly change. She just grew up, and now she pretends that she's a good Christian, and that all her former sins have been wiped away, forgotten. But that's not true. I remember everything.

"I'll be over tomorrow, hon." Krissy waves as she turns away from me. "Come, Ada," she hisses to the child, who is following along behind her, with wide eyes. I feel badly for her.

I sigh, shaking my head. I turn away, only to find there's a man smiling at me. He's dressed in a button down and dark slacks, a leather jacket on over top instead of a blazer. He's good-looking in a devil-may-care way.

"I see Krissy found you," he says. I squint. He seems familiar. His eyes widen. "Don't tell me you've forgotten me."

"I can't believe it. Horrorshow?" I'm speechless—his jaw is chiseled enough to cut glass with. His lips are pouty, sultry in a masculine way. It's disgusting really, but he's a tall glass of something cool and he knows it.

"Yeah." He grins, and I can see the remains of the kid he used to be. "I moved back to town a little while ago." I decide to store this information up for future use.

"Stacia won the art contest drawing your portrait as a pig," I recall. He no longer has those round, pink cheeks. They've hollowed out in a way that would have disappointed my best friend.

He laughs, throwing his head back. He nods, rubbing his jaw. "On a motorcycle. A Harley. Yeah. I deserved that. Stacia was... they broke the mold after they made her, didn't they?" He smiles and it's like a thousand-watt bulb has been turned on. Perfect, straight teeth. Blue eyes that sparkle. I bet he's a heartbreaker.

I'm smiling genuinely for the first time. "True."

"What have you been up to, Olive?" He looks at me closely.

"I'm a mortician." I swerve the conversation away from my father. I don't want to break down in front of this man. He can't be trusted. Once a bully, always a bully.

"Really?" His brow arches.

"It pays the bills," I say. "Plus, I don't get talked back to."

He laughs, eyes wide as if he's surprised to find my gallows humor funny. He nods, squinting as if he's seeing me for the first time.

"You're not afraid of ghosts?"

"Not even a little," I reply, leaning in. "Though, they try to grab my toes when I sleep."

Our eyes meet, and we both laugh. I'm relieved to have a reason to laugh. My guard remains up, however.

"Sorry about… your dad. I hope they find him." His smile falls. Clouds cross his eyes like the sun.

"Me too." This is sobering. He's genuine when he says it.

"How are you holding up?"

"I'm hanging in."

"Are you going to be in town long?"

"For the foreseeable future."

"If you need anything, and not casserole," he says. "I live down the street too. Your dad and I went fishing a few times."

"You did?" I ask, but I don't press. I have to admit, I'm a little jealous. If he had time to fish, he had the time to drive up to Nashville to see me and chose not to.

"Yeah. I moved back in with my folks after my wife divorced me." There's pain in his eyes. "Your dad got me out of the house. He's good people."

"He is. I'm sorry to hear that." The trauma is still there. The scars, though invisible, still retain their shape. I cannot trust him, nor fully warm up to him. In my mind, he is still the cruel child he was two decades ago. It suddenly occurs to me: he might have information. "Do you know something?" I whisper.

He leans in. "Not here," he says, glancing around anxiously. I smell his cologne. "But we have a lot to talk about."

"Well, I'll see you around," he says, raising his voice. He's looking at me pointedly, and I realize that he does know something. And he's afraid to tell me here, in public.

"I'm sure you will. I'll be around the house, waiting for news." My heart is racing— he's not the sort of person to scare easily. He nods, his mouth a grim line. I return the gesture, my stomach doing a nervous flop. Turning away from him, I walk through the crowd, then I go and wait in line. My mind is reeling.

The room smells of the flowers. Lilies, for the most part. Perfume. All covering up the scent of embalming fluid and decomp. When I get to the front, I step up to the casket, kneeling on the riser. Whoever worked on her did a good job. Her face has a healthy peachy glow to it. Her lips are a pale pink.

"Thank you," I whisper because I never told her in real life. Despite my years of experience with death, I'm tearing up. So many missed opportunities to thank the people who have gotten me through life. Have I ever thanked my dad? He always called me Cool Customer. I know I'm not great at showing affection. I haven't been open since Stacia vanished. Fear colors my every move.

I sniffle, then I move on, making my way out to the bright, fleshy pink foyer. I sit down on a bench. Across from me, there's a large gilt-framed mirror. My eyes are watery. My own face blurs.

I remember a conversation with Miss Bradbury. It was right after Stacia's disappearance. I'd been drifting through school. I had to be there—but I wasn't. Not really. Over and over, I fixate on what I remember—and what I don't.

Stacia, walking a little way in front of me, as we climb downward into a gully. That's where the cave is, the one she vanishes into. After that, my memories end, until a flashlight is shining into my eyes.

"Olive? Can you stay back a moment?" Miss Bradbury asks, breaking into my thoughts. I nod, coming suddenly out of a drift.

"Ooooh," Horrorshow says in a high-pitched tone. "Olive's in trouble."

"Mr. McCallis," Miss Bradbury warns. Horrorshow smirks at me. I stare back at him, unsmiling. I've recently perfected this. It's clear that it works—my psychiatrist tells me it's unsettling. The smirk falls from his face, and he looks away quickly.

I lean back into my desk chair while everyone else gathers up all their things. I glance out the window. Snow is just beginning to fall. It's mid-December, right before Christmas break. Stacia has been gone for almost two months now.

Once the others have gone, Miss Bradbury sits down across the aisle from me. She smiles, her eyes softening. She's dressed in green and black gingham, with a rust cardigan. Her hair is swept back in a bun. Her lipstick is a perfect cherry red. I stare back at her, waiting to hear which spiel she's going to give me.

While Dad has been quiet, silently placing little gifts into my coat pockets when I'm not looking, my teachers all seem to believe that I'm one stern pep-talk away from being completely healed.

"I know you're going through a rough time, with losing both Stacia and your mom," she says, unsurprisingly. She's not the first to give me this talk. "Your school work isn't going so well. I'm willing to let a few things slide, but you have to meet me halfway."

"What's the point?" I ask, although I'm intrigued she's not giving me a dressing down, like my other teachers.

"I know it seems like it's really hard, but you're going to survive this," she tells me.

"I guess." I've lost the person who understands me the best. It feels like Stacia is everywhere and nowhere at the same time. After that night in the woods, I feel different. I no longer feel safe in crowds. It's like all my senses are on overload. I can feel what other people are thinking. "I don't really want anything."

"What's going on?" she asks. "What's really going on? You're too bright not to want anything." When I look into her green eyes, there's understanding there. I don't just see it—I feel it. "I know what's it's like," she says softly. "To lose someone who helps you feel like the best version of yourself."

My throat tightens as my vision blurs. That was the thing I truly needed to hear. She's lost someone, too. In my mind, an image of a young man floats up from the darkness. I can see him, lying in a casket, dressed in a soldier's uniform.

I hear breaking glass, metal. Cars, crashing beneath a dark, star-spangled sky. I understand, or at least, I have an idea.

"I can't remember what happened that night," I say, finally giving voice to the deep guilt I've been experiencing. "Not a thing. I want Stacia back, but it's like my brain's been wiped clean. I'm the only one who could possibly bring her back, and I can't remember anything." A large, warm tear slips down my cheek. "I feel like I've betrayed her."

"No, Olive," Miss Bradbury says, looking into my eyes. "It's not your fault. It's the person who took Stacia. It's their fault." No one else has said this either.

I nod, but it does nothing to assuage my guilt. My heart is pounding in my chest. The world blurs at the edges. I know, on one level, that she's right. But inside, I have the overwhelming feeling it is my fault.

If I hadn't agreed to go into the woods. To continue going to the cabin, then Stacia wouldn't have been in the woods that night. It is my fault. And it's even worse that I don't remember. If I could, then perhaps Stacia would be here now.

My stomach does an awful twist, and I can feel bile rising in the back of my throat as I see the young man, lying on the ground amid the broken glass, blood leaking out of him. His face is a pulpy mess, and his arm is at an odd angle. His eyes open, in my mind. They are black orbs. *Come Home, Olive*, he says.

"Thank you, Miss Bradbury," I mumble. "I have to go." Picking up my bag, I run down the hallway, bursting out the door and into the sunlight, where I throw up in the bushes.

CHAPTER NINE

2024

THE SOFT STRAINS OF THE PIANO BEGIN. I don't want to stay for the service. I've done what I needed to. I've paid my respects. If Miss Bradbury is lingering, then no doubt, she's heard me. When I glance in, I see that Krissy is sitting next to Horrorshow, Ada between them. He glances over at me, raising an eyebrow.

I turn and leave, not stopping as I move through the door. I keep walking, traveling through town. My heels click on the sidewalk, and I bury my hands in my blazer pockets. My purse hits against my hip. It's all familiar, but it's been a very long time since I last took a walk through Blackwell. The few times I've been back, I stick close to Dad's. In the years following Stacia's disappearance, we avoided the woods or talking about them. Only now does that seem strange. He was avoiding talking about them. So, how long has he been trying to find Stacia?

I walk past the new shops. Blackwell's main street has a few high-end fashion boutiques. There's a coffee shop, an ice cream parlor. Just at the end, there's the post office, and the high steeple of the church.

My heart pounds as I make my way to the entrance to the woods. It's loud in my ears as I go down the path. My hands are in fists. The visitation I had last night was pointed. It knows I'm in town.

The path is cracked and stony. It hasn't been kept up over the years, simply because it isn't much used. No one goes hiking out this way. If they do, then they'll go to the National Park that's a twenty-minute drive. I've been there—the woods feel different there. Less watchful.

There's a darkness in the Deeping Woods. It permeates even the air. I'm breathing heavily. I should have worn sneakers, or at least sensible shoes. As I leave the path, my heels sink down into the dark, wet dirt.

I pause, my knees feeling a bit weak. I feel like I'm playing chicken. I stand there, willing myself not to move. I can't go any further. Not too much further into enemy territory. Once you leave the path, then you have to play by its rules. I wonder what I need to do to wake it up. I want to demand it to give Dad back.

Nothing has changed in the Deeping Woods. They look the same as they did nearly two decades ago, when I came here with Stacia. The only thing that has changed is me. I nervously push my hair back behind my ears. It's sticking to my face in the heat.

It's quiet at first. Not even the birds are singing. It's so still, like something's watching me, waiting for me to make the first move. Suddenly, I hear it. I would have thought it was the wind, but there's not even a breath of it. All around me, I hear voices, whispering. Many voices, in a language that I can't remember.

It causes goosebumps to rise over my arms. Through my clothes, I can feel the touch of cold fingers, running down my spine, it's almost like a greeting.

I feel a presence, behind me. That familiar tingle at the back of my neck.

"I've been waiting for you," Stacia says, her voice still that of a twelve-year-old girl. It's almost like she's standing behind me. Just like the myth of Orpheus. I know if I look back, she'll vanish. "Why haven't you come sooner? I missed you."

My mouth is dry—cottony. I lick my lips. "Have you taken my father?" I ask, not entirely sure I'm talking to my best friend, gone these past twenty-four years.

"He came to me," the voice says, now deeper. Rasping with age.

"Give him back. I'm the one that you want." My heart is racing, my palms sweaty.

"You are." It's the thing that lives out here, and it might be using Stacia's voice to get to me. Nature made the anglerfish; she also made whatever lurks in the Deeping Woods.

"Where do I need to go?" I ask.

There's no answer. My heart beats faster. I feel it, getting closer. I can feel the shadow of the hand that's about to clamp down on my shoulder. I can feel its breath, cool on the back of my neck. I don't want to look, but I do.

When I turn around, I am alone. I feel like the trees are pressing in all around me. The whispering starts up again. A cold thrill travels across my skin. Sobbing, I turn and run, back down the path, back to safety.

CHAPTER TEN

2024

MY FEET MOVE, TAKING ME OUT OF THE forest. It isn't long before I find myself standing in front of the Kessels' house, only a few doors down from my dad's on Banks Street. The yellow paint is peeling. All the aging blinds are drawn. One of the shutters hangs askew, and there are green shoots, growing out of the gutters. The foliage is creeping in, the bushes and the grass growing wild around their house.

I wonder why they never left Blackwell. With a jolt, I realize—they're still waiting for Stacia to come back home. I've given up, but they haven't. I feel like a traitor. I haven't spoken to either Mr. or Mrs. Kessel in years, avoiding this house during my rare visits. Now, it's time. Whoever took Stacia is back. Taking a deep breath, I walk up to the front door and ring the bell.

There's a long silence. Eventually, I hear the soft sound of footsteps nearing. The door opens, and I'm face to face with Stacia's mother. Gray streaks her dark hair. Her face is deeply carven with wrinkles around the same dark eyes as Stacia. She's wearing a gray sweater and jeans. She seems surprised to see me standing there.

"Olive," she says. "It's been a while." This was the woman who filled in for my missing mother, for a time. Once Stacia vanished, everything was broken. I couldn't be a stand-in for her missing, vibrant daughter. No one could.

"It has. I… was wondering how you and Mr. Kessel were doing."

She smiles, though it falls immediately. There's pain in her eyes. "I didn't expect you to come… I…"

"Do you still blame me?" I ask, pain lacing every word as I remember the last time I saw her, at Stacia's memorial service. Standing in front of an empty casket, the smell of funeral flowers sweet in the air.

"I should have never said that to a child," she admits. I feel like I can breathe again, though I blink back tears. She smiles, her eyes glistening with tears of her own. "Won't you come inside?" She steps back, holding the door open for me. "I can make tea."

"Tea sounds lovely." It's comforting, in a time when I crave comfort. I can tell she's lonely, too. That she needs to talk to someone.

"Come on in," she says. My lips curve upward.

I step inside. I haven't been here in ages. It's the same, but older. Less alive than it had been all those years ago. It has the same scent of rose petals and spices it had when I would come over to hang out with Stacia. Though still decorated in marigold and pink with dark hardwoods, it's threadbare. Dusty. And very quiet.

"How is Mr. Kessel doing?" I ask, noticing that the house feels empty. The television is silent. Usually, whenever Mr. Kessel is here, the television is on. He's an avid watcher of what he calls "soap poppers."

"I recently had to place him in a nursing home," she says. Mrs. Kessel seems like the life has been slowly seeping out of her, and now I know why.

"I'm sorry to hear that," I say, feeling awful for not checking in. I should have come sooner, but her anger at Stacia's memorial service seemed like an emotion that would never cool. I felt guilty, for being the one to come back.

"It happens," she says, leading the way down the hall, to the kitchen. "I wasn't able to afford to keep him here after he had the stroke. In-home nurses are very expensive. Please, have a seat. Is there any news of your father?" She fills two mugs with tap water, which she then places in the microwave.

"No. Not that I've heard." I've been checking my phone, disappointed when I see nothing. It's been forty-eight hours since my father's disappearance. The chances they're going to find him alive are rapidly dwindling.

Mrs. Kessel nods. She looks me in the eye. She knows how it is when someone has gone missing. Just as I do, too. The absence has a presence of its own, an ache and a darkness.

"Did he say anything to you? My dad?"

"He said a lot of things," she says, looking down at her folded hands. They're knobby, gnarled. "He comes over often. Ever since... Stacia." She exhales, covering her eyes with her hand.

"I know that he was trying to find Stacia," I whisper.

Mrs. Kessel visibly tenses, her gaze lifting as her hand drops to her lap. "I told him not to. Whatever is there in those woods is evil. Whatever—whoever—you girls found out there should just be left alone." She leans forward, imploring me. "You know that."

"I don't remember what we found," I admit, my mind going back to what I do remember. Stacia, entering a cave, the darkness swallowing her up. Then, a blank, until I came to hours later, wandering muddy and barefoot through the woods alone. "I have—fragments of memories. Whatever it was—when it showed its true face—I don't remember." I swallow around the jagged lump in my throat.

"It's probably for the best. Some things just aren't meant to be messed with. After all, there's more on Earth than is known or recorded. Your mind's protecting itself. As much as I would like to know where Stacia is, perhaps it's better if you don't remember."

I let out a deep breath. What I recall of those strange months leading up to Stacia's disappearance are scattered. They seem like a movie I saw once and barely remember. It would help if I did. But I think whatever was in that cave excised itself when it expelled me and took Stacia. "I think I need to remember," I whisper. "To save Dad."

Mrs. Kessel nods. We both sit, staring at our hands in silence. She gets up when the microwave beeps. She busies herself with putting tea bags into the mugs.

"We used to think of you girls as two sides to the same coin," Mrs. Kessel says, a sad smile coming to her face—I can hear it in her tone, her back to me.

I smile at the memory. Stacia, with her dark chestnut hair and eyes. Me, with my red-gold hair and pale blue eyes. Opposites. Light and dark. Stacia, so bright and energetic. I was the one who revolved around her, a minor satellite. Mrs. Kessel places a steaming mug with a Lipton tea bag in it on the table in front of me.

"You know, I never understood my girl," she says as she sits down, the chair creaking beneath her slight weight. "Whenever I looked at her, she seemed to me a changeling. I somehow knew that someday she wasn't going to come back to me because she didn't belong to me at all. I feel like I failed her. But you didn't. You understood her."

I blink back tears, staring into the depths of my mug. My own mother would have said the same about our relationship. For the first time in ages, I feel my mother's loss, keenly. "Stacia understood me," I say, thinking of Mila, and how wrong I was about her. "She's the only person who ever did." No one understands you as much as your childhood best friend.

We're both silent for a moment, both of us lost in our thoughts. I can hear the soft ticking of a clock, somewhere nearby. This house is quiet. Too quiet.

"He had so many questions the last time he was here," she murmurs. "I wish I had seen it for what it was."

"What did my father ask you?" I ask. I don't want to cry, and I'm holding back tears, trying to stay brave.

"He wanted to know if Stacia had left anything behind. Any clues as to where she went. I told him that she didn't. If she did, then I didn't know it."

"Did he say why?"

"He said that it was because whatever happened that night still haunted you. He said that he wanted to finally set you free."

I know I've gone pale. I exhale as I cover my face. He went into the woods for me. To slay whatever monster lurks there. Of course. Dad is my protector. Suddenly, our last conversation clicks into place.

I stand up. "I—I should go."

"Olive," Mrs. Kessel says, and I look at her. "If there's anything—anything at all, I want to help. Your father has been a good friend to me. And you were my Stacia's only friend."

She's speaking as though Stacia is dead. To Mrs. Kessel, perhaps she is. The daughter who is never coming back. I still hope that Stacia is still alive, somewhere in the woods, just like my father. If she didn't die that night, I will find her, no matter how awful it is for me to return.

"Thank you. I'll let you know when I know more." I grip Mrs. Kessel's soft, worn hand. Hold her gaze for a long moment, as long as I possibly can. "I'm so sorry." I then walk to the door, letting myself out. I make it to the sidewalk before I start crying.

CHAPTER ELEVEN

2000

AFTER FINDING THE CABIN, STACIA AND I return the very next day. Immediately, we check the results of our offering. The milk and cake are all gone. The bowls are empty. Beside it, on the table, there is a little bundle of meadowsweet flowers: white puffs, their green stalks tied together with a bit of purplish string, and beside them, a gray stone with a hole in the middle.

Stacia and I share a look. Our offering has been accepted. Just the fact it's gone, and there are these strange items in its place, indicates someone or something has been here.

"A hag stone," she says, picking up the stone, peering through the hole. "Now, maybe we can ask the Fae for help in finding the girls." She puts the stone into her pocket. Later, she will wear it on a string around her neck.

"What's it good for?" I feel like I have a sugar rush. This is the most exciting thing to ever happen to me. Whenever Stacia is around, interesting things happen. But this is proof of something other—something bigger than either of us.

"It's good for seeing through enchantments," she replies. I wish there had been two. Then, I could have had a hag stone, too. But Stacia's the special one. She'll know how to use it. "Let's get to work."

We begin to clean up the cabin. We start by carrying out the debris, putting it into a pile outside. As we pick through it, we find things—a burnt thimble, the remains of a handmade quilt, a bent fork. I am digging through the detritus when I find a locket.

It's tarnished, but ornate. I hold it in the palm of my hand. It's the size and shape of a songbird's egg. Flowers and vines decorate the surface. The chain it should hang from is broken, as if it had been torn from someone's neck. It, too, is darkened with age.

"Look at this," I say. Stacia walks over. She puts her hand over the locket, then pulls it away, gasping as though she's been burned.

"Open it," she says, curiosity seeping into her voice.

When I open it, there's a picture of a woman on one side, a baby on the other. The pictures are protected by a layer of foggy glass. The woman's hair is old-fashioned. Her collar is high. The baby is in a white, lacy dress.

"I think she lived here," Stacia says. "With her baby."

"She's beautiful," I murmur. I have the strangest sensation I know her. That I've seen her before.

"We need to leave it here," she says. "It belongs to her."

I nod, placing the locket up on the mantel. Stacia has placed a handful of holly boughs, held together with twine up there. All of it together, with the skulls, it looks witchy. This place is starting to feel like a home for us.

"This is a much cooler hideout than Horrorshow and Johnny have," I announce.

"Yeah." We've spied on their hideout, which is a little treehouse in the backyard of Horrorshow's house. This is way cooler. No one will come out here. "Look. The floor is stone." Stacia scuffs her shoe against it.

"That's good." On our way here, we talked about what we would do if it needed repairs. After all, neither of us know much about woodworking. I've seen my father do a few things around the house. However, I wouldn't be able to do it on my own. "We should get a lock, for the door."

"Maybe, someday, we can get paint," Stacia says.

"Purple?" I don't really have to ask. It's our favorite color. Both of us have painted our rooms lavender, with the very same paint.

"Absolutely. Come on. Let's have something to eat." She says it half-heartedly, as though her mind is somewhere else. I frown, but I grab the shopping bag. If it's important, then she'll tell me when she's ready.

We both sit down at the table, where we pull our sandwiches out of the bag. This is the last ordinary moment we have together. Neither of us knows it.

"I wonder who the woman in the locket was," I remark as I chew my tomato and cheese sandwich.

"She was Old Witch Annabelle," Stacia says around a bite of her peanut butter and banana. "The people of the town hated her. Even more after her baby went missing."

"How do you know it's her?" Everyone in town knows about Old Witch Annabelle. She killed her baby, even though she claimed she was taken by the fairies. It feels unreal that we would find her cabin, still standing. It's ancient history.

Stacia shrugs, tilting her head to one side as she chews, swallows. "I can feel her here, still."

"What else can you tell me about her?" I wonder, gently pressing Stacia's strange talents. I'm curious to know the extent of them.

She tilts her head to the side a little more. Wrinkles her nose. "She's sad. Wait…" Stacia stands up. She goes over to the fireplace, where she kneels. "Olive, help me."

I go over to where she's kneeling, trying to pry up one of the hearthstones. I get up, and grab the flathead screwdriver I brought. Together, we pry it from where it sits, flush against the stones around it.

It comes up, and we struggle to lift it. Underneath, there's a wooden box. Untouched by the elements, kept safe from fire, water, and time.

We bring it over to the table. It's covered in dust. I swallow the lump in my throat.

Stacia opens it. There's a leather-bound diary. It's old, the pages wrinkled and yellow. When we open it, it's written in a language we don't recognize. Symbols that are strange.

"What does it say?" I ask. Stacia shrugs, sets it aside, then lifts out the piece of paper beneath it. She unfolds it, gently. The paper makes a cracking noise as it's opened.

"It's a map of the Deeping Woods." I note the Snake River, the town of Blackwell. It looks like the cabin is marked with a crude drawing of a house, as well as a bunch of X's, in black, smeary charcoal.

"A treasure map?" Stacia wonders.

"I think she was looking for her baby," I reply, pointing at all the X's. "These are the places that she looked."

"I wonder what's there," Stacia mused. There's a red circle, around the middle of the Deeping Woods.

Recalling all the maps of the area I know of, I say, "It's the caves system. It runs beneath the mountains. There are abandoned mine shafts which tap into them."

"What?" Stacia looks at me with respect. For once, I know more about something than she does.

"There's a map of them at the Historical Society," I explain. "There's a cave system that runs all the way through Appalachia. Part of it goes through the Deeping Woods. Not to mention, the old mine shafts tap into them at certain places."

"So, it's all hollow?"

I nod. "There are old stories about the things that live inside of the caves," I tell her. "My Dad's collecting them as a part of his job."

"So, if we asked him…" She raises her eyebrows.

"He would tell us everything," I assure her. "What do you think is here?" I ask, pointing to a spot on the map. It's blank. Far from any of the trails, which are marked out on the map.

"Let's go see," she says, standing up. She pauses, at the doorway. "I wonder…"

"What is it?" I hardly know what to expect.

"Will you help us?" Stacia calls out. "What's hidden in the woods?" We stand there in the doorway, and I have the strongest feeling she's been heard. There's rustling in the leaves, all around us. As though tiny feet are moving through the dry detritus. And, whispering. I panic, my skin crawling.

"Come on, Olive." Stacia takes my hand as she begins to walk forward. My feet are frozen in place, causing her to stop and turn towards me.

"What is it?" My stomach twists nervously. The rustling is only growing louder and louder. We're surrounded. I can't see anything.

She tugs my hand. "Sometimes, you just have to trust them, Olive," she assures me.

"Who?" I feel like I'm standing on top of the high dive at the Orange Avenue Pool. Except instead of cool, aqua blue water for me to plunge into, there's a deep, dark pit with no bottom in sight.

"You mean, *what*," she replies. That's even worse. All my senses are telling me we're in grave danger. But Stacia's not afraid. And I believe in her. She's waiting patiently. I sigh, letting all the air in my lungs out before I nod. Stacia turns, and together, we walk out of the cabin and into the woods.

Stacia leads the way off the path. I swallow, but I don't stop walking. We're covered in bug spray, and we both have hiking boots on. We're heading downward, into a gully. We go all the way down, until we're standing at the bottom. Stacia stops, and then we wait.

I glance up, where the trees seem to grow upwards for ages. The summer sun and a gentle breeze are filtering through the leaves. I watch as a cloud passes overhead, blotting out the light. When I inhale, I smell the scent of oncoming rain.

I'm holding Stacia's hand in a death grip. If she weren't here, then I would never have come this way. All around us, we hear more whispering. I look at Stacia, who is looking all around us. She's smiling. She puts her finger to her lips.

"Look," she whispers, pointing.

As she does, a golden light is floating towards us, through the woods. It's growing dark now, all around us. Raindrops begin to fall, but Stacia walks forward, towards the light. I take a deep breath, and together, we follow the golden ball of light deeper into the woods.

It makes its way forward, floating on the air. Rain is falling steadily, now. As we go deeper into the woods, there are more and more lights. They float towards us, and then around us. I feel a deep sense of wonder. I've wanted to experience magic, and here it is. I've found it, dwelling deep in the woods. The one place I've been warned away from.

Stacia holds up her hand, letting one alight on her palm. I follow suit. It's warm, buzzing softly against my skin. I feel a warmth, emanating in my chest. "What is it?"

"I don't know."

"It makes me feel... good." I'm scared, too, but will never admit it. I can hear whispers, coming from the dark foliage. They're just out of sight. When I try to look right at them, they retreat.

"I wonder who the whisperers are," Stacia says. She's beaming. "I wonder where they're leading us."

"Me too," I say, playing along. Apparently, we're surrounded. Though I'm terrified, I'm also enchanted at the same time.

"Do you think they want us to go to that cave, Olive?" Stacia asks. I look up to find there's a large yawning cave, right in front of us.

"Maybe," I say, my stomach lurching. This is not a good place. In the distance, I can hear water, dripping. I have vertigo, and the sudden feeling I've been here before.

Standing at the entrance, there's an outbreath, as if the cave has just exhaled. It smells of damp rock and something else. All the hairs on my arms are standing up. I look over at Stacia, who's squinting into the darkness. "Well?"

"It feels… old." She speaks slowly, as if she's probing the depths of the cave. "Let's at least go inside, to get out of the rain." I can't help but shiver. A coppery taste is at the back of my throat.

"Okay." I hope we're not going too far inside. I feel like there's something watching us. Like a spider, waiting for little flies to get stuck in its web. I wrap my arms around myself. I'm drenched through from the rain, and there's cold air emanating from the cave. My hair and clothes are stuck to my skin. Goosebumps are rising all over my arms.

As we walk inside, Stacia reaches into her pocket and pulls out a tiny Maglite, which is as slim as a pencil. She twists the top of it, turning it on. Inside, it's quiet, except for the sound of water, far off, and our footsteps. I think I can hear voices, whispering in the distance.

"Do you hear that?" I whisper, the sound of my voice echoing in the vast space.

"Yeah."

"What are they saying?"

"I can't tell. Come on, Olive. Let's go in further."

"No, Stacia." It's the first time I've ever denied her anything. I'm terrified of what lies deeper inside this cave. My stomach roils with dread, much like when I dream of the thing in the skin suit.

In the little light, I watch her turn towards me, her brows drawn together. "Why not?"

"We don't know who—or what—those voices are," I whisper. "They might be the ones who took Jackie Morton." We have no weapons. No way to protect ourselves.

"Then we'll be quiet," Stacia hisses. "This is the most exciting thing that's happened to us, Olive." When I don't respond, she purses her lips. "You stay here. I'll go further."

I grit my teeth. "Okay. I'll come." Staying here by myself is somehow a worse thought than going in. She smiles, then leads the way. I force myself to follow.

Our boots make crunching noises in the dirt. All around us, there is darkness, except for the slim beam of Stacia's flashlight. The walls seem to narrow the farther in we go. There's a point that pinches inward, which we both squeeze through. Stacia goes first, then I follow. When I make it to the other side, Stacia's standing still, letting the frail glimmer of her flashlight travel over the room.

Way up, at the ceiling of the cave among the stalactites, there's a hole, and light filters through, giving the room a bit of ambiance. Raindrops fall inside, pattering on the floor. At the center, there's what looks like a long stone box, about the size and shape of a roughly hewn coffin. The walls are high, and the floor is soft dirt.

"What is it?" I whisper. I can hear the voices, coming from *inside* of it. Calling out to each other. Dread is rolling through me in sickening waves. Whatever it is, I do not like it.

"It feels asleep," Stacia remarks. My stomach curdles as Stacia steps towards it, her boots making a soft padding sound in the dirt.

"Stacia," I whisper. "Don't." It feels like we're trespassing. I watch as my friend's pale fingers, almost glowing in the dark, continue to move towards the slab, slowly, inexorably. When Stacia's hand touches it, we both feel it. Something in the dark, opening its eyes.

My knees go weak as I feel it, taking stock of us. I have never felt so small and frightened in my entire life. It's like staring into a great abyss, one that looks back and judges for itself.

CHAPTER TWELVE

2024

I OPEN MY EYES. I'M LYING ON MY CHILDhood bed, staring up at the ceiling, which is covered in warm, golden afternoon light. I've cracked the window open, and the soft sound of the wind in the trees fills the room. It's warm, but I shiver. That cave. That was not the last time Stacia and I went there. There's more, but all the memories are coming back to me slowly. I have to go through them all to get to the one that matters most. The main piece of the puzzle, where it sits beneath a snarled tangle of detritus.

If I keep going, I will eventually make my way back to something I have already faced. I have the strongest feeling that, whatever it is, only one of us will walk away. No, I don't know who—or what—my adversary is. I roll over to glance at my phone. Nothing new. No word from the police.

I sit up, slipping my phone into my pocket. I'm still dressed for the funeral, but my shirt is untucked, my shoes abandoned at the side of the bed. I need coffee, and then I need to come up with some sort of a plan.

I walk downstairs to the kitchen, where I fill up the coffeepot. Once the pot is burbling merrily, I slip my phone out of my pants pocket, and dial Mila.

"Milway Family Mortuary, Mila Milway speaking," she says. She's using her calm voice, the one that's reserved for bereaved family members. Beneath that honey-smooth veneer, I can hear the brittleness. She's used to speaking with people who are upset.

"Hey Mila. It's Olive."

"Olive! How are you?" She's still using that tone for the bereaved. Although, I suppose it's warranted in this case. I'm just not used to it being pointed at me. I know there's more. Hopefully, it'll be left unsaid.

"I'm hanging in there. How are things there? Do you need me to come back?" I have to offer. We're never short of work, and there are only three of us.

"Have you found your father yet?" She responds with a question, and I love her for it.

"No. No word." I bite my lip, torn between wanting to be needed, and wanting for someone else to take the dark journey into the Deeping Woods. I've never told Mila the whole truth about Stacia. She doesn't know how bad things really are.

"Don't get me wrong, we need you," Mila says. "We're really crunched. But you have to look after your father. Family first, you know?" It's the Milway Family Mortuary's slogan. I snort, and Mila laughs.

"Thanks," I say.

"No problem. Are you okay? Are you—holding up? And I mean really," she says. I know that she's leaning back against the counter, down in the basement.

"I'm trying to keep it together." My voice is small, and my vision blurs with more tears.

"Do you..." I hear the hesitation in her tone, and I know what's coming. "Do you want to talk about what happened? I know it wasn't what you wanted to hear, but—"

I remember baring my soul to her. I had thought she returned my feelings. After all, there had been a drunken kiss, after a holiday party. One that apparently didn't mean anything at all. As a matter of fact, there's someone else.

"No. No—it's fine. I understand." I can't demand feelings from her that don't exist. There's a long, pregnant pause. I know that she's biting her lip.

"Okay. Well, if you need someone to speak to, I'll be in the basement all night. I've got an accident vic who needs his face rearranged before his family shows up at ten tomorrow."

"I'll keep that in mind." She's trying to revert to how we had been. I don't know if I'll ever be able to get there. Not entirely. When I jumped, she didn't catch me, leaving me to shatter on the ground.

"Really, Olive," Mila says. "I know it's not what you want, but if you need to talk, I'll be here. I'm still your friend." Mila's the closest friend I have. I wish I'd told her more about Stacia, so I could add everything else. But now's not the time. She's busy.

"Thank you. Really. It's good to hear your voice."

"Yours, too." I hear the smile in her voice. I feel, for the first time, comforted.

"I'll let you get back to work," I say. After we both hang up, I find I'm at a loose end. I could call Johnny Bowen to check up on the investigation, but to be honest, I know he doesn't have anything. He's looking for a normal explanation—that my dad's gotten lost in the woods. Or, that a human was the perpetrator. He's not looking for anything... supernatural.

I have nothing to do, so I go downstairs and haul out the vacuum. Dad's big on keeping the house clean. He'll be relieved to find it just as he liked it when he gets back home.

If he ever gets back home, Stacia's voice says in my mind. I don't like the smug tone in her voice. I feel a cool breath on the back of my neck. My hand snaps up, and I turn, but there's no one there. I stand, frozen.

In front of me, the air seems to move—like when the asphalt is hot during the summer. It's in the shape of a woman though she's clear. Her long, spindly fingers reach out towards me, and my head suddenly aches, in a thin seam down my forehead. My heart pounding, I reach out. I feel menace, rising from her. As my fingers go through her, she dissipates. When I blink, there's nothing there. Shaken, I switch the vacuum off. The room is blurred through my tears. I inhale and exhale in sharp bursts, my hand on my chest.

The doorbell rings, startling me back to reality. I inhale, wiping at my eyes with both hands as I walk to the door. When I open it, I find Krissy, still dressed in bright colors. She holds out a foil-wrapped glass dish. Behind her, Harley's there, wearing jeans and a black t-shirt. There's also the small girl, standing silently to the side. Ada, a miniature version of Krissy.

"I brought you my famous cheeseburger and noodle pie," Krissy says, pushing it into my hands. I accept the warm dish, surprised to find them here. I glance under the foil to find a layer of cheddar cheese over what looks like a queasy mix of beef, egg, and macaroni noodles.

"And I brought some beers." Harley holds up a six pack of Samuel Adams. My Dad's favorite. It's even the Octoberfest. Which means he's been drinking with my father before. I have so many questions. I curse Krissy for coming over now.

"Thanks for coming," I say, trying not to stare at the beer. My eye catches Harley's. His lips quirk upwards, his eyes widen. It's a sign—he's done it on purpose. My curiosity is piqued. "Come inside. I just put some coffee on."

"That sounds great," Krissy replies, pushing past me in a haze of some sort of expensive perfume. She drags her daughter in after her.

"You can sit down in the living room," I tell them. "I'll just go put this in the fridge." My mind is reeling. What am I even supposed to do with them?

IF you had ever told twelve-year-old me that I would be sitting in my father's living room with Krissy Bradshaw-Bedecker and Harley McCallis, then I would have laughed. As it is, it's awkward. We're all sitting, sipping from cups of coffee, except for Ada. She's sitting, her small hands folded in her lap. She's calmer than Krissy was at that age. Somber.

"So, Olive," Krissy says, drawing my attention. "I know that you're probably looking for some guidance in these troubling times."

"Not really," I murmur, sipping my coffee. Guidance, no. Help, yes.

"Well, I spoke with Pastor Daniels at our church, and he says that you're more than welcome to come to our prayer group. We would like for you to attend, so we can all pray with you."

I take another gulp of my coffee, while I come up with an answer for this. "Thank you," I begin. "That's a kind offer."

"One we hope you'll take us up on," Krissy chirrups. "Right, Ada?"

The girl looks worried. I look away from her, and into Krissy's over-excited gaze. I'm confused. This whole scene is odd. I glance over at Harley, who grins at me. He's enjoying this, I realize.

"Thank you," I lie.

"You can come too, Harley," Krissy adds.

"I'm still a skeptic on the whole God thing," he replies flatly. Krissy looks horrified. I try not to laugh, covering it with a fake cough. He looks right at me. "So, has your father spoken to you about the goblins?"

"Not in some time," I reply. To be honest, I'm surprised that Harley clearly has. He grunts. I have a lot I want to ask him, suddenly. But not in front of Krissy, who is here on a church mission. We're all silent for a very long moment. Krissy is frowning deeply— this isn't going the way that she hoped.

"Well, Ada and I ought to get going," Krissy says, setting aside her coffee cup. "I have cookies to bake for tomorrow night's PTA meeting."

"I'll show you both out," I murmur, following them to the door. Krissy's got a firm hand on Ada's slim shoulder. The girl looks down at the ground between her feet, clad in black Mary Janes. There's something familiar about her, but I can't put my finger on it.

Krissy turns towards me as we reach the front door. She smiles at me, sadly. "I'm so, so sorry about your father," she says, almost as if he's dead.

"I'm hoping he'll turn up alive," I say drily.

"Well, if you need anything," she begins as Ada walks down to the sidewalk without her. "I know we were never *really* close, growing up. But I think, if we tried, we could be." It's too little, too late. I can't say this, though.

"Thank you. Thank you for the casserole." I glance out to Ada, who has turned around. "It was nice meeting you, Ada." She nods, once. There's a curious gleam in her eyes. Her brows knit together.

"You're welcome," Krissy says. "And don't forget the prayer meeting—it's Wednesday night at seven."

She smiles brightly, then traipses out through the door, calling to Ada as she crosses the lawn. I close it softly after them. I have the strongest feeling Krissy assumes I'm going to show up. Christians always try to help, but always miss the mark. Prayers and magic are two different things, after all. Asking versus manifestation; it's a big distinction.

When I go back to the living room, it's empty. I hear the sound of a beer being opened—a hiss. When I turn, Harley is holding out the opened bottle. He has another, pinned between his upper arm and his body.

"Do you believe her?" he asks.

I take the proffered beer, the bottle cool to the touch. "Not really. It's hard to change your entire personality, even if she did have more than twenty years to grow up."

He grins, laughs. "Smart." I don't add what I want to say about him. Old resentments simmer beneath the surface of my skin. We go back into the living room, where we sit down on the couch.

"So, did your dad ever finish his book, about the Kentucky goblins?" he asks.

My eyebrows shoot up. "Not that I know of," I reply. "He hasn't spoken of it—not after the exhibit at the Archives was considered a town joke."

He sighs, leaning forward, so his elbows are on his knees. "Olive. I need to level with you."

"Okay." I take a gulp of beer as I steel myself for whatever it is he's got to say.

"He didn't stop working on the book. He was working on it last week when I came over," he says.

"You hung out with my dad?" My mind is processing this. Why didn't Dad ever mention he was spending time with Harley McCallis? Moreover, why didn't he tell me about the book? A memory flares in my mind—his face, the night of the exhibit disaster. I am surprised to find I'm jealous, that my father wanted to include Harley, but not me.

"Let's just say that I had an interest in the goblins," Harley mutters in a low voice, then takes a swig of his beer, hissing a little. I stare at him, my mouth hanging open.

"Who are you?" I demand. The whole town laughed at my father for his exhibit. He was crushed when no one believed his theory. As far as I know, he had given that up for less controversial town history.

Harley smiles, and I can see the child that he used to be—the one who proudly called himself Horrorshow McCallis. "I have been preparing for something like this my entire life."

"This isn't a horror movie, Harley," I snap, my hand clenching tightly around the bottle. "This is my father's life. He's in danger."

"Oh, I'm well aware," he says, looking me coolly in the eyes. "It's your life, and my life, and Stacia's too." I stare at him for a long moment. I realize Harley's here to convince me to go with him to find my dad. "I know that you know what I'm talking about. That there's something out in those woods, and we have to go in and stop it." He takes a swallow from his beer. I stare at him, completely at a loss. In a way, I'm relieved because I won't have to go into the woods on my own. The way he's gulping down that beer, I know that he's terrified, too.

"Okay. You going to explain?" I ask, settling back into the cushions. This is going to be a long evening. He grins, clearly pleased that he didn't have to convince me. He's going to get the surprise of a lifetime when it's finally my turn to talk.

"Absolutely," he says.

I glance at my bottle. This beer is nowhere near strong enough. I need something harder. "I think we're going to need something stronger. We'll talk in the kitchen. Dad has a stash of popskull, I think." We both get up, and then walk towards the kitchen.

CHAPTER THIRTEEN

2024

HARLEY AND I SIT AT THE KITCHEN table. I've got his bottle of whiskey that his good friend Soren Willis makes. I stare at the bottle, wondering if Soren might know anything about Dad's disappearance. The amber liquid sloshes against the glass, catching the light. Another thought, for tomorrow perhaps.

"There was another part to the exhibit," Harley says. "One that he didn't use because he didn't want to upset you."

"The one with the missing children?" I ask. I've seen it. It's in the basement.

He nods, running his fingers through his hair. "Yeah… unfortunately."

"Great. So, most of it's in the evidence locker in town." I look at him. "Do you think you can convince Detective Bowen to do us a favor?"

"I might," Harley muses. "We used to hang out sometimes." This is intentionally vague. I narrow my eyes to slits. A slow smile spreads across his face. "He's the sort of person who crosses all of the t's and dots all of the i's, you know?"

"Makes his bed twice before he gets in it?" I mutter, wondering when they had a falling out.

He nods, raising his eyebrows. "And then makes it again. Although, I'm sure that between the two of us, we might be able to convince him otherwise."

I nod. He's put us on one team. This is good. But I just wonder what he's doing here. I mean, Harley McCallis was on his way places back in high school. Last I heard of him, he had gotten a good scholarship to go to Duke University. He left but somehow ended up right back here.

We're both silent for a very long moment. Something's bothering me. After all, I'm here because I went into the woods. Stacia and I trusted that thing that lives there. I know Dad started noticing patterns, within the town's historical records. Whatever he found, drove him out there. But why's Harley here? I decide to be as direct as possible. I pour out two shots, slide one across the table to Harley. I knock mine back. "What happened?"

"What do you mean?" he asks, his eyes on the shot glass. The way the light is falling on him draws out the sharp angles of his face— the way his undereye area sags from lack of sleep, the deep lines scored into his forehead.

"What brought you to come ask an aging town historian about his exhibit of proof in cave-dwelling creatures?" I ask. He laughs, a sharp bark.

He sighs, takes his shot. "I met my wife in college. We… got pregnant by accident. Got married, almost immediately. We were kids. We barely knew each other. As soon as Dahlia was born, though—" He sighs. I can see the weight of his grief, how it presses down on him. "Everything was perfect. She was perfect. She made us better.

"It was when we were here, visiting my parents," he says. Suddenly, I know how this story ends. "My daughter went missing seven years ago. She was… she was standing right next to me. I looked away one moment… and she vanished."

"I'm so sorry." I really do know—the ache, the not-knowing, the loss—I've been there.

"Dahlia went missing without a trace," he says, sniffing as he wipes at his eyes.

"When?"

"October 29, 2012."

"In Blackwell?" I'm trying to think back. I was in college. Getting my degree in mortuary science. I was in a disappointing relationship with another future mortician, a man who had more interest in the dead than me. Looking back, it was a disappointing time in my life. Dad may have mentioned it in passing, or—maybe he didn't tell me at all, because he didn't want me to get upset. Which is more likely.

"Yeah. When we were visiting my parents," he repeats. His brow is furrowed. "One moment, she was there. Next moment, nothing. Vanished. My wife—ex-wife—no longer talks to me. She blames me, also she thinks I've gone completely insane."

"So you thought goblins?" I ask, thinking about how far into left field he's gone to reach this conclusion.

He looks at me significantly. "Your father told me that you and Stacia called them the Fae." A cold, hard knot forms in my chest.

"Yes." I hadn't realized how much my father might have overheard of our talks. He was there, listening in. Probably smiling as he heard us discussing magic and ritual. Our ideas on the missing children. He knew more than I suspected. My eyes dart over to where the children's cookbook is wedged between the sugar bowl and the wall.

"I think you know more," he prods, gently. My gaze slips upward. I note those dark circles underneath his eyes. That haunted look—of someone who has lost someone. I need to put aside what happened when we were children. This is my only ally, and I need him, if I want to find Dad before it's too late.

"I do. And I don't."

"Explain, please." He's imploring me, as a father who has lost his daughter. I think he knows that he's talking to a daughter who's lost her father. A girl who lost her best friend.

I pour us both two more shots, take mine before I speak to dull the pain and worry that I'm feeling, causing tightness in my chest. "I only remember parts. I can't remember most of the night Stacia vanished. Whatever happened, it's completely gone from my mind. I'm beginning to recall parts of the summer before, and I've got all the winter after. But..."

"They took them," he says bitterly. He takes his shot. He hisses. "They take everything—to hide their tracks."

This is a good point. I pour us both two more. We're both silent for a very long moment. Harley is the first one to speak.

"My wife has moved on," he says. "She has another husband, another family now. I have… nothing. Just this big hole in my life. I've been working as a paranormal investigator. We help people, like clear evil spirits out their homes. But… there's not a lot of money in it. I'm living at my parents' house. You know, I lost the one person who looked at me like I was worth a damn." He sighs, shaking his head. "She was just a little kid." He sniffs, shakes his head.

"Believe me. I get it."

"I know you do." He looks me in the eye. His are watery. For the first time ever, I think I actually see Harley McCallis. The person he is, underneath all the swagger. It makes me sad, like I'm seeing him naked.

"I need to remember," I tell him. "Otherwise, we won't know what we're up against. I mean, we can guess, but… if I can remember, then we might actually have a chance."

"True." He nods.

"Harley, did my father tell you where he was going?" I ask.

"No. As far as I know, he went looking for more clues," he says, tapping his shot glass against the table as he talks. "He would often go into the woods, to just… poke around. But he never said that he was going to approach… whatever is out there. I think he ran into them, by accident."

"Or they were watching him," I add before I even think. His eyes snap up.

"You seem…" His eyes narrow, and his mouth hangs open as he tries to complete the sentence. He rubs his chin with a hand, closing his mouth, pressing his lips together in a grim line.

"I faced it before and came back. I know that this time, I might not walk away," I tell him. "But if I can stop it, save my dad, save anyone else, help you find the answers that you're looking for… that's what matters." He nods, his eyes are wary. He doesn't know I don't have much of a life to go back to.

"I'm searching for something, but I don't know what," I say, staring down at my hands. "Drifting through my days on a sea of emptiness, feeling like a large part of me has been excised with a scalpel. I wonder if this journey into the woods—into my past—will help me get it back."

"Cheers," he says grimly, pouring us out two more shots. Our eyes meet. We clink glasses, then down them. I've got a nice buzz, winding its way through my veins. However, it doesn't get rid of the overwhelming feeling that we're both in a lot of danger—that tightness in my chest, a knot, is twisting even tighter beneath my sternum.

It's like we're two prisoners on death row. Two soldiers, going into battle. When I look into Harley's eyes, I see he feels the same way. We're both facing our doom. But we're doing so for the people we love most, who have been taken from us.

Because we both believe they can be saved. A fool's hope, but hope, nonetheless.

CHAPTER FOURTEEN

2000

THERE, IN THE DARKNESS OF THE CAVE, that very first time, Stacia and I stand there, staring into the abyss. The darkness seems to turn towards us. It was large, ancient—the smell of dirt wafting on its icy breath. Some type of cold light catches the moonlike tapetum lucidum in its eyes. Then, it recognizes us. It's an odd sensation. I'm both terrified and welcomed at the same time. While I've read so many stories about the Fae and magic, I've never experienced it like this before.

There's the sound of rock breaking and sliding, as the door opens. The stone table is not a table. It's a doorway, downward and into the earth. The large creature in the dark is a watchman of sorts. Its fingers are like roots and shadow. Stacia and I both enter—there's no going back. Only forward, along the dark stone hallway.

There are no lights. Nothing. Just cold darkness, the sound of our boots scuffling the stone floors. We make our way by keeping our hands on the walls. My heart is pounding in my chest. We don't know whose hallway this is. Or even what lives down here.

The floors are worn from the passage of feet. They are smooth, with barely any rocks at all. I reach out, running the flat of my palm along the wall, which is smoothly carved. I can feel the ridges where someone has scraped it even with a tool. Someone's hands made them, carefully. They have been here for a long time. I can feel the weight of it, pressing in all around me.

"Wait," Stacia says. "There's a door." There's the sound of creaking hinges to my left. I place my own hand on the door, and I feel old, softened wood. I blink, because suddenly, we're surrounded by light. I feel a strange vertigo.

"We shouldn't be here," I whisper.

"But we are." There's a smile in Stacia's voice. We're standing in the cabin. It's whole, unburned. None of the signs of age or the woods encroaching upon it. The light here is warm. Late autumn reds and golds. It seems like a fairy tale cabin—brighter, more robust. There's a warm fire, burning in the hearth.

"How?" I gasp, looking at the crisp, fall leaves that are strewn across the stone floor. The bed, with its soft mattress is made up, a hand-sewn quilt spread across it. In the bookcase, there are leather-bound books, neat gilt writing on their spines.

Stacia laughs. "Does it matter?" she asks.

I smile, laughing with her because it doesn't. Not now. Not when we're in this magical place, where the light is golden. I feel it entering me, settling in the pit of my stomach, like a warm sun. When we walk out through the red-painted door, the woods are filled with bright amber lights. All the lights float on the air like bubbles.

"They're here," I murmur.

Stacia holds up her hand, letting one of the lights lands in her palm. It's a round orb, which tinkles like a bell. "Hello," she says.

"Were these the voices we heard before?" I wonder, placing my hands over my stomach. For the first time, I can feel the raw power—the potential within myself to effect change for something greater.

When I reach my hand out, I watch as my palm begins to glow, changing as I think commands: *gold, red, purple.* It's inside of me. It has always been inside of me, but it hadn't been until we went through the gate that I can find that power and bend it to my will. I kneel, and then pick up an acorn from the ground. Stacia is watching everything I'm doing with interest. The golden fairy lights bob and weave in the air around her. They keep changing from gold, red, purple, and then back again, as I request.

Turning my focus inward, to the acorn on my palm, I straighten up to my full height. The acorn shifts. I will it to begin to sprout. I feel the large ball of light rise to the center of my chest. A great sun, at my very center. Its warmth and light flows through my veins, out through the palms of my hands.

I blow, watching as it floats, landing and then growing into a small tree. It continues, growing larger and larger. Golden leaves begin to sprout from the branches as they spread outward.

"Olive!" Stacia says, impressed. "That's brilliant!"

"You try."

"Okay." She picks up a handful of leaves, and then suddenly, they're all floating in the air, glowing golden. Stacia holds up her arms, twirling around. I follow suit, and we both laugh as we spin.

Fairy lights and the leaves, float all around us. The world seems brighter than it's ever been. Possibility and intention combine. I feel alive and awake—all my senses are heightened. I can hear my heartbeat, the sound of the wind, the lights as they make their bell-like music.

I stop, suddenly. What if—what if we're still down in the caves? What if this is just a dream? Or worse, it's something else's will? My stomach makes a roiling flip. Everything seems to turn into a photo negative—black and white ghosts.

Stacia grabs my hand, pressing it tightly. Our eyes meet. Her irises are gold, glowing with power. My anxiety goes away. If we're back in the caves, then surely, I wouldn't feel her touch like this, or the warmth of the wind on my cheeks. My best friend looks me in the eyes.

"No one can know about this place," she says.

"No one," I agree.

"We'll make a blood oath," Stacia says. She just finished reading *The Oak Mage* for the first time and has been talking about the blood oath ever since. "Then we'll be sisters. Real sisters, like we've always wanted."

A slow smile spreads across my face. "Yes." Even as I breathe out the word, this too is effecting a change. It's a magic word, and it causes something inside of me to open. We open the door to the cabin and find ourselves back in the cave. This isn't accompanied by the same fear I felt only a moment ago.

We walk down the hallway. It's so silent, cold. I feel eyes, from further down on us. Behind us, I hear the soft patter of a footstep. I glance back to see two glowing eyes, down the hall, watching us go. I feel the power still flowing through my veins, keeping me from feeling any sort of fear.

As I watch, more eyes open. Small, pale creatures in the dark with luminescent skin. I can hear the soft patter of many feet. The slow, even breaths of many beings. We are at the head of a parade of many cave-dwellers. Who they are, and what they want with us, I don't know?

We step out, past the dark void of the gatekeeper, with its long, slender fingers. I turn to look, to see if those who follow us will step out, into the light. The door is closing behind us—there's the sound of stone, scraping against stone as the way through is shut. The Watchman turns over, and goes back to sleep, sinking down into the darkness. We know, however—if we return this way, we will be welcomed back. I can still feel the ball of light in my chest. Something that lay dormant within me has been awoken. It feels good.

It feels like the presence here has agreed with us. Oddly, this presence feels female, unlike the Watcher. She's not in this cave, but somewhere nearby. She has watched us, this whole time, waiting. We have passed her test. A blood pact is acceptable to her. She likes the idea. Both of us can feel an image being communicated with us, in our minds.

The full moon is like a silver coin in the night sky, dark clouds floating slowly past it. This is when it will be best for us to do it. I glance over at Stacia. For a second, as we step out of the cave, her eyes look like two black orbs, but when she blinks, it's gone.

∾

HOLLOW GIRLS

THE next full moon is two weeks after our first foray into the cave. We spend those two weeks in intense planning for it. First, we had to find a blood oath. The only place we find it is in a fictional account of the life of Morgan Le Fay—Rowena Pennyworth's *The Oak Mage.* As two teenage girls in Kentucky, it is incredibly difficult for us to find any real how-to manuals on this sort of thing—real magic.

We both tell our parents that we will be sleeping over each other's house. We meet at the end of Banks Street, then plunge into the woods, backpacks and bedrolls hitting our backs. We laugh and run, throwing our heads back to howl up at the orange-sherbet sky.

We are strong. We are one, as we make our way along the familiar trail that leads to the cottage in the woods. When we arrive, the sun is setting behind the trees. We set out a battery-operated lantern, then close the door, putting on the padlock we bought at Ace Hardware. We feel safe in here, insular.

Stacia takes out the things we've gathered, setting them out on the floor that we've scrubbed clean. I unroll my bed roll, sitting down on it.

"We'll do it at midnight," Stacia murmurs. I glance out the window, watching as the sky fades to a pale purple. I shudder a little. Chills run down my back, excitement pooling in the pit of my belly.

Once everything is set out, we begin to set a fire in the fireplace. We cook hot dogs for our supper, and eat them, sipping from cans of warm Coke. Here, in the flickering glow from our fire, we both feel safe, full and happy. Here we wait until midnight, talking.

"What do you think will happen?" I ask Stacia.

"I don't know," she replies. "Anything could happen." That's exactly how I feel. We could go anywhere from here. That raw potential we both discovered within ourselves in the cave—we're about to harness it, to bend it to our will.

Together, we weave handfuls of meadow sweet and sunflowers into flower crowns, which we place on our heads. Slowly, we go from lanky pre-teens to powerful priestesses. We put on white cotton dresses, preparing ourselves for the magic which we have come to perform. Real magic.

When Stacia's alarm goes off a few moments before midnight, I glance out of the window to find the round disk of the moon, staring down at us from the sky. It hovers over the treetops. For the first time, I can feel its presence overhead. There's a dark magic emanating from it. A beautiful buzz, sparkling and fizzling through my veins.

This is real. This is the most real I have ever felt in all my life. It's as though I've been asleep for twelve years, cocooned in the safe confines of Blackwell. It was the moment Stacia and I stepped out, into the woods, into the cabin, then finally, into the cave, that I woke up, stretching out my wings.

Stacia opens the book, weighting the pages with two stones. I glance at the mantle, where the locket and the skulls stare back at us. The hunting knife is set out beside the book. I catch Stacia's eye, and she smiles.

"Ready?" she asks.

"Yes."

She exhales, picking up the knife, and reading the directions from the book. "Make a prick over the clavicle," she says. "Then, we drink a drop of the blood." Her eyes meet mine. This is a moment of communion, unlike any other.

She steps towards me, knife in hand. Her eyes are on mine, as she makes a slim cut over my collarbone. I barely feel the cut, only the softness of her lips, the gentle flick of her tongue as she licks a drop of my blood. When she's done, she straightens, licking her lips.

She hands me the knife. My hand doesn't shake as I make the cut on Stacia's collarbone. I lean in, my lips brushing against her skin. Using my tongue, I taste the iron of her blood. The strangest thing happens. As I straighten up, my eyes meeting Stacia's, it feels as though the world flips.

I feel a rush I've never felt before, a closeness with Stacia that is deeper than the close friendship we've had for years. In the darkness, her eyes seem like black orbs. Her lips are red with my blood. I reach out, touching her lips with two fingers.

We're both grinning as she touches her fingers to my lips. We are bonded in a way that can never be broken. She leans in, pressing her lips to mine. We are two halves of the same coin. We laugh, grabbing each other's hand as we both pull apart. This closeness is what I will seek, but never find again.

Golden light catches her dark hair, her darker eyes. I can see myself, reflected there. The light to her dark. Two sides of the same coin.

"Come on," she says, leading the way. The lock is already opened, and we run through the door. We're barefoot, dressed only in the thin, cotton dresses—flower wreaths on our heads.

We run out and into the woods, where the Fae surround us. We spin, in a dizzying dance. Both of us look upward, where the moon is silver through the branches. The Deeping Woods are alive, all around us. The golden lights suddenly surround us, as their whispers grow louder. Stacia laughs. I notice we're surrounded by figures dressed in dark, ragged, and hooded robes.

"You can see them now," she says, grabbing my hand.

"I can see them," I agree, looking around and seeing their pale bodies, their round faces, their oily black eyes as they peer out at us through the bushes. They look like children.

Stacia grabs both of my hands in hers and we begin to twirl in circles, drunk on our new-found power. We're both laughing, our heads thrown back. They don't come near us. They just stand quietly, whispering to each other. Watching us as we dance in circles in the woods.

WHEN I wake up the next morning, we're snuggled up together. The door to the cabin is wide open. I see something in the doorway. I get up, disentangling myself from Stacia. When I look down, there's blood on the front of my dress, causing it to stick to my body.

I keep moving, towards the door. The air smells fresh, clean. It rained sometime in the night. Sunlight spills through the branches of the trees. At some point, it rained, and small droplets are still cascading from the leaves. Cicadas sound all around me.

There, on the ground, are two little sewn figures. Soft, like cotton. I kneel, picking it up. One has dark hair, the other, red. They're lovely.

Only then, do I recall—silent figures, watching us. Only now do I experience fear. What—who—are they? Looking around, in the light of morning, there's nothing there. We have stepped out of the safe, cozy suburban world of paperbacks, bicycle bells, and into the darkness, into the secret edges of the world. Into the forest.

I reenter the cabin, with the poppets in my hand. There are vibrations coming from them. They don't feel bad. When I smell, there's a gentle, herbal scent. I recognize rosemary, lavender.

Not knowing what to do, I put them into my backpack.

Stacia stirs, groaning as she turns over. Her eyes open, just a crack.

"Olive?" she murmurs.

"Yes?"

"What time is it?"

I check my watch. "Eight."

"Let's go get breakfast at the diner."

"Yes, let's." I don't know why I don't share the poppets with Stacia. It feels like something that was left for me, although I don't know why. Stacia's the special one. I'm just—I don't know what I am.

We change out of our blood-stained dresses, balling them up, then sticking them in one of the ramshackle cabinets in the cottage. As we walk through the woods, lost in our own thoughts, Stacia reaches out, takes my hand.

"Now," she says. "Now we're blood sisters."

I grin. "Like we always wanted."

"No one will ever be able to separate us," she says. I nod.

"Last night was incredible. I've never felt so…"

"Alive," Stacia finishes.

"Free," I say, finishing my thought as I had wanted. My stomach growls. My appetite has never been so big before.

"Yes," she agrees, though she's frowning.

We arrive back in Blackwell and go straight to the diner. We order full breakfasts, eating ravenously. We do not talk—we don't need to. I know what she's thinking, feeling. Being there, amongst all the other diners, I feel changed. For the first time, I do not belong among the people of Blackwell.

CHAPTER FIFTEEN

2024

HARLEY AND I HAVE MOVED BACK INTO the living room. He's put on *Hellraiser.* The bottle of whiskey is sitting on the coffee table, in a state of near depletion. I feel warm, content. This is likely the last time I will ever feel this way again. I can't deny I needed this.

As tipsy as I am, I can't lie to myself. That Dad is still fine. It's been forty-eight hours, and his time is running out. A small voice inside of me says that he's still alive, somewhere out in those woods. I have to go there, but I have to work up the courage to do it.

"This is stupid," I say, "although the way that he's melting through the floorboards is pretty impressive."

"Oh, come on! It's a classic," Harley insists. "Or, you know, if you want to watch something newer, we could watch *MIDSOMMAR.*"

"Are you going to tell me *MIDSOMMAR* is a classic?" I ask doubtfully.

"Are you trying to tell me that it's *not*?" Now that he's been drinking, the Southern twang has entered his speech—he says "tryunatell." He quirks an eyebrow and purses his lips. We both stare at each other for a moment. I grit my teeth, trying not to laugh at the face he's making—he looks just like his mother. She's been the gym teacher at the middle school for about thirty years.

"It was stomach turning, and that's saying a lot because I'm a mortician. I have seen so much fucked up shit," I say.

"Ari Aster created something so uniquely terrifying, in broad daylight!" His eyes are wide, baring the whites.

"It was gross. I couldn't eat for nine hours." The lurid technicolor acid trip of the Hårga and the flowers made everything so much worse. The screaming, the flames. I look over at him, and our eyes meet.

"I mean, people don't get horror," he says, gesturing with his glass. "It's not necessarily about scares. It's about the human condition, social anxieties, you know? *MIDSOMMAR*, for instance—fear of other people."

"What about *Nightmare on Elm Street*?" I ask, mostly to keep him talking. Anything to avoid the reality of my own situation.

"Fear of being attacked when you're at your most vulnerable," he replies, shrugging. "When you're asleep, you know." There's a twinge at that thought, as I think about last night. *Welcome Home, Olive.*

"I guess I can't argue with your logic." I'm thinking of my own fears. At the moment, it's the fear of the unknown—of what I know but have since forgotten. Of discovering something I don't want to know again. It's a cold stone in the pit of my stomach. *Welcome Home, Olive.* That figure, pulling back from the window. I recognized that figure, almost. A memory lingers just out of reach, then vanishes.

"Wait, so what is the most fucked up shit that you have seen in real life?" he asks, his eyes wide with open curiosity. I laugh, nervously. I can't tell him the truth about that. Not now, when the sun is going down outside.

"I used to drive the pickup van," I say, leaning my glass against my lips. "Had to go and collect the bodies, bring them to the mortuary. Not everyone needs an autopsy, not all deaths are suspicious, and often, they were still laying wherever they'd dropped. This man was stuck… in a tree. I guess, he'd fallen off a balcony, but—he'd ended up upside down. He'd been there awhile, and well… really decomposed."

"Weird." His eyebrow is raised. He's staring at me, intently, and I have to look away. My cheeks are warm.

"Yes." I take another sip, the whiskey burning down the back of my throat.

"Can I ask you a question?"

"Shoot."

"Why'd you decide to become a mortician?" he asks.

"I guess… I guess I wanted to help people, you know—on the worst day of their lives. They've lost the person that was important to them," I tell him. "And I help them get through that day, to say goodbye." I finally look over at him.

Harley's smiling at me crookedly. There's a ruddy glow to his face. His stubbly beard rasps as he rubs it with his hand. He's looking at me, like he sees me. The thing is, he doesn't—not really. He's only seeing the human side. The one that's logical. There's another part of me, one part that I've buried beneath this façade. One that knows how to use magic. One who is bonded to Stacia in a way that can never be broken.

I wonder how he'd look at me if I told him the truth. I don't have an answer to that. I still don't really trust him. Not to mention, I'm a little jealous my dad trusted him.

"You know, I would have laughed," I say. "If someone had ever told me that we'd be sitting here, like this." I let my gaze return to meet his. "Like friends."

He blushes, looking at the glass in his hands. "I'm sorry, Olive."

I look at him sharply. Suspicion fills me like a cold faucet. "For what?"

He looks at me. "For how I treated both you and Stacia. I was an asshole for a very long time. The truth is, the two of you were so much cooler than the rest of us. You were both so real. And you didn't care what other people thought… and then Stacia was gone. And you were completely checked out. I should have… I don't know. Seen if you needed a friend."

I look away from him. My throat is tight, my teeth are grinding together hard. I don't want to say something angry. He had so many chances to make things right, years ago.

"It's not an excuse," he goes on. "I should have been kinder. I learned the hard way that that wasn't the way to be. I wish I'd seen that and been there for you."

I look at him. I nod slowly, as a hard knot within me begins to loosen. What's the point of holding grudges? Honestly—he's the only help I'm going to get. He's lost someone too. "I don't really forgive you for being a jerk, but you're okay now. It's Krissy who's still insufferable."

"All Krissys are insufferable." We both laugh.

"True."

"Did you and Stacia really practice witchcraft?" he asks.

"Yep."

"Really?" To my surprise, he's impressed. The truth comes tumbling out of me.

"We did a blood oath," I tell him. I can still recall it—the rush of it. Those strange, hooded figures in the woods. Did we dream them, or were they real? The memory of them makes my heartbeat hard against my sternum.

"Huh," he says, nodding, raising both eyebrows in a mixture of surprise and respect. "You two were way too cool for Blackwell."

"Yeah, we were." A smile curves my lips upwards. *We still are,* Stacia says in my head. I think back to that warm golden light, inside my chest. A feeling I have not experienced since Stacia's disappearance. Grief, welling up inside of me, overflowing with cold, dark water.

"Do you think we'll have to do witchcraft?" he asks.

"Before this is over… it's highly likely." After all, that's what worked then. I can only imagine that nothing's changed. It requires an exchange. A sacrifice to get past the door.

"I've dabbled," he admits. "I have dabbled."

"Really?" Now, it's my turn to be impressed.

"I was ready to turn to anything to bring Dahlia back," he says thoughtfully. "Nothing worked. Not God, or Satan, Thor or Hekate... nothing and no one." He shakes his head. "I think you're the last person I have left."

This was much how I felt about Stacia. It's also time for me to share what I know.

"The Fae—or goblins or whatever it is out there," I tell him. "It doesn't play by those rules. They'll need something from us in order to give something back. That's how it works."

"I figured." He says it tiredly. I can see how the grief weighs upon him. He rubs his chin, his hand rasping against his five o'clock shadow. "What sort of a thing?"

(*Blood*). I'm not sure where the thought comes from. I get goosebumps, though. It's in a female voice.

"Not sure," I say. "But we'll know it when it's time." This is when my phone rings. The number is withheld. I quickly pick up. My heart plummets upward, into my throat.

"Hello?" I'm expecting to hear the voice of Detective Bowen.

"Olive," Stacia says. My eyes shoot over to Harley, who frowns. Hands shaking, I put it on speaker.

"Stacia?" I say aloud, my mouth going dry.

"Why aren't you coming?" she asks. I watch as Harley's eyes widen, and he goes very pale. Clearly, he's caught off-guard. Of all the things he was prepared for, this wasn't one of them.

"Coming where?" I ask, though I already know.

"Into the woods," she says, sounding angry. "Why are you hanging out with Horrorshow? Don't you love me anymore?" Her voice goes gravelly, like she's speaking with decomposing vocal chords. I feel a chill sink down into my bones. Goosebumps cover my arms and my legs. I can see the mouth it comes from—gray lips, dirty, jagged teeth.

"How do I know that I'm talking to you?" I ask. "And not the thing that lives in the woods?"

(*Her*).

"I think you know, deep down inside. In the part of you that you let die," Stacia says, in her gravelly dead-thing voice.

"That part of me hasn't died," I say, my eyes on my phone. The number on the display is blinking out, turning into random numbers and symbols.

There's crackling as the connection fails. Stacia laughs like dry leaves rustling. When she speaks next, her voice is sad. "Come home, Olive. We need you here." There's crackling, then I hear a woman's voice start to speak in the background, but the line goes dead.

I look at Harley. He's pale, his eyes wide.

"Have you been getting calls like that for a while?" he asks.

"Ever since my dad went missing," I say. "Ever since I came back to Blackwell."

"I never thought that I'd hear her voice again," he says, rubbing his face. "I… can't quite believe I'm awake."

"I'm just relieved that you heard her. I thought maybe I was imagining it."

"No. You're not," he assures me, his eyes wide. "What—I don't—" He shakes his head. "Where has she been all this time?"

"In the woods," I say, my gut feeling leading me to this conclusion. We're both silent. Harley pours us both another shot.

"I feel like I've stepped through a portal," he says.

"Welcome to my life." We take our shots, forgoing any sort of toast. Stacia's not dead. She's been alive, all this time. I just want to know—why hasn't she come for me before? I was here, for the final three years of high school. I've been back a handful of times. Why now?

I turn my eyes back towards the television, but my mind is outside, in the woods. In the darkness that resides there, waiting for me to return.

CHAPTER SIXTEEN

2024

I'M IN THE DEEPING WOODS, WALKING barefoot. The mud is cool beneath my feet. The woods are full of a fog, rolling in. The sky overhead is sunless, gray. When I look down, I'm wearing the dress that I wore the night Stacia and I made the blood oath. But I'm grown up—not a twelve-year-old child.

My dress is dirty, a far larger amount of blood marking the front of it. The wound on my chest is fresh, blood slowly seeping through the fabric. Touching two fingers to it, they come away, stained red. When I look up, standing in front of the cottage is a woman I haven't seen in a very long while. I stop, my feet rooted in place.

There's something wrong with her eyes. "Come home, Olive," my mother says. She's wearing the dress I last saw her in—kelly green, but now ragged, torn and dirty. Her blonde hair is wet, shaggy. Her feet are muddy.

"You're the one who left," I snap. I'm afraid, but also angry with her. She purses her lips. As I watch, her eyes become two dark holes.

"Come home, Olive." Her voice is raspy, as though her throat is dry, like wheat, rattling in the wind. Her eyes turn black and oily. The peach tone seeps out of her skin, until she's pale.

"I am home," I reply, my heartrate rising.

The monster laughs, baring teeth that are sharply pointed. "No, your real home, Olive. *With us.*"

I blink, and suddenly, she's right in front of me. Her abnormally long, dirty fingers grasp my wrists. "Come home," she growls, her voice low as she leans in. "*She's* waiting." My heart is about to burst from fear.

"Who? Who is she?" I ask, but she opens her mouth, a shrill scream coming out.

I come awake with a start to find I'm still on the couch in Dad's living room. Harley's stirring. The television and lights are still on. I must have made a sound.

"What's wrong?" he asks me sleepily. He sits up, rubbing his eyes.

"Nothing," I say, my heart rate slowing. I'm sweaty, almost like I'm sick. "It was just a bad dream." The Deeping Woods are calling out to me. Whatever is in them wants me too. It's greedy. It takes and takes without giving anything back. She. She takes, whatever—whoever, she is.

He stretches, looking at me blearily. He sits forward, inhaling. "I should get home."

"You can stay." It's out of my mouth before I realize it—I'm afraid to be alone in the house. If it can get into my head like this, then I don't know what will happen. For a moment, I think of *Nightmare on Elm Street*—the fear of something attacking you when you're at your most vulnerable.

"Really?" Harley asks, his brow arching. I blush a little, embarrassed by my fear.

"Yeah," I say, looking him in the eyes. "Neither of us should be going out alone after dark. Use the couch. I'll go upstairs."

"Fair enough." He pulls the afghan off the back of the couch, spreading it over his legs.

"Hey Harley?" I murmur, folding my arms.

"Yeah?" He stops what he's doing to look at me.

"Thanks for being here."

His smile is genuine, though it doesn't reach his eyes. "No problem, Olive."

"Goodnight," I whisper, then I walk upstairs. He doesn't respond right away.

"Goodnight," he calls after me. I can hear him turn off the lamp with a click. I'm relieved I have someone here with me. Even if it is Horrorshow McCallis. In a way, he's prepared for this. It's his battle too.

Without turning the lights on, I get into my bed, the sheets cool against my skin. Staring up at the ceiling, I think back to my dream.

I'm still shaken, and how the thing in the woods can take the face and voice of whomever it wants. My father was trying to release me from its hold. Whatever it was, its long-nailed claws are still digging into my psyche. *She.* She's waiting. I have the overwhelming feeling that whatever she is—she will never let me go.

∾

I'M next awoken by something climbing onto my bed. It's still nighttime. The window is open—I can feel the air, cool on my cheek. I open my eyes to find Stacia leaning over me. Her teeth are pointed, and her eyes are dark pits.

She smells of dirt, mushrooms, moss.

"What are you?" I ask, panicking.

She smiles, her eyes still furious. "I'm Stacia." It's a mockery. Too raspy, too deep for a twelve-year-old.

"You're pretending to be Stacia." I stare into its eyes.

"Ask me something only Stacia would know." She says it proudly.

"What book was the binding ritual in?"

"*The Oak Mage* by Rowena Pennyworth," she replies, her icy fingers brushing against my collarbone. In the place where we are bonded—where I still have the silvery print of a scar. "Wake up, Olive."

Hot tears spill down my cheeks. I reach out, cupping my best friend's cold cheek. She's no longer human.

"What happened to you?" I ask because she's not what she was. But I can feel the bond—that glowing space inside of me. The part of me that I believed died with her. It's still alive, ticking like a watch.

"I've stepped out of time," she says. She takes Olive's hand. "Come with me. We'll travel the paths where no other human has gone." She sounds like something demonic.

"I can't. Not yet."

"Your father doesn't need you anymore." This is not what I wanted to hear. Stacia would never ask me to give up on my father.

"What?" I wish this was her, but I don't think it is. I don't think I should trust it.

"No one needs you but me." Her teeth are jagged, gray. And her eyes are black pools. In terror, I see the hag stone on the lanyard around her neck. I reach out, grabbing it. The creature Stacia pulls away, screaming inhumanly. I feel the lanyard strain, then break as she slips towards the window.

My eyes open. I'm standing by my open window, unbalanced. Almost as if I'm about to fall. The long drop to the ground yawns beneath me. I catch the windowsill with my available hand. My other hand is clasped around something cold and hard.

As I come all the way awake, I lean back, landing on the floor with a heavy thud. I'm breathing heavily, a coppery taste in the back of my mouth. I hear feet, running up the stairs, and I panic for a moment, until I recall Harley was sleeping on the couch downstairs.

"What's happened?" he asks.

"There's something here," I gasp through my tears. I'm freezing, though it's August.

"What?" Harley looks around wildly, placing his hands on the sill, then leaning out of the window. I scrabble to get up.

"Who is that?" he asks as I lean out, as well. I look where he's pointing. There's a tall, slim figure, out on the lawn, staring up at us. It has long, dark hair. Its legs and bare feet are dirty. It's a vague approximation of Stacia. The dark hair is blown across the face. It's too dark to really see her. She's wearing a mask, made of a deer's skull whitened by time. The antlers are uneven.

Blood calls to blood. In that moment, I know that it's Stacia—what's left of her. She raises her hand, waving to me. I clutch at the window, to stop myself from jumping after her.

Suddenly, she turns, then runs away into the woods behind the house across the street, melting into the darkness. She becomes a part of the darkness.

"Olive—who—what—" He stops, just as flabbergasted as I am.

"Stacia," I say. I'm looking down at my hand. I'm clutching the hag stone, which is on a broken lanyard. The lanyard has become brittle with age, which is why it broke when I grabbed it. The sight of it is confirmation of something. I think whatever it is, it was once my friend. She has become something—unhuman.

In a daze, I look over at Harley. He's standing there, staring at me. He's frightened; I can see the whites of his eyes, the tension in his mouth.

"What does she want?" he asks. I know the answer—it's a feeling in my gut.

"She wants me to go with her." Cold dread pools in the pit of my stomach. My hands shake with fear. I'm staring down at the stone in my hand.

"Where? What's in those woods, Olive?"

"I don't know," I sob. "But for a moment, I almost went." The truth is, I miss my friend. More than words can express. I just don't know if she's who she used to be, or if she's become something else entirely.

Harley wraps an arm around my shoulders. I let myself be comforted. His scruffy chin leans against the top of my head, and he pats me on the back with the flat of his palm. He smells human—of sweat, sour breath. I let myself fall apart, even as I clutch the hag stone—incontrovertible proof. My sobs are the only sound. The night is quiet, completely still. As if everything that lurks in the dark is watching, waiting.

CHAPTER SEVENTEEN

2024

THE NEXT MORNING, HARLEY AND I ARE sitting quietly across from each other. The coffeemaker is on. The house smells of toast and coffee, bacon. Ordinary smells, which anchor me here. Neither one of us wants to discuss what happened last night.

Harley stuffs a slice of bacon into his mouth. As he's chewing, he speaks, "Okay, Olive. Now, tell me. What is it that you need to do? Like, to remember?"

This is a good question. A valid one. I stare into the depths of my coffee mug.

"I'm not quite sure," I reply. "Whatever it is, it has my father. So…" I trail off. Panic is flooding my veins. In my mind, I see the cave, and Stacia vanishing into the darkness.

"It's been here, for a long time," he says. It's an inference. "The woods have always been dangerous. Even my grandparents said so. Whatever it is, it's old."

"And powerful," I whisper. He raises an eyebrow, waiting for me to explain. "It has magic, of a kind," I tell him, running my finger around the rim of the mug. "It's…" I sigh. "Stacia and I made contact with it."

His gaze is steady, his blue eyes boring into me. "How much do you remember?"

"Not enough." Stacia, walking into the cave. Never to come out again. My throat tightens.

"What if we had you hypnotized?" he asks. I blink at him. No. I don't want to give up control. I picture a scalpel, slicing into my skin. Peeling back the layers to autopsy my lost memories.

"I'd rather check the archives," I mutter as my stomach does a nauseating flip. The thought of remembering is not a good one. There's a reason I don't remember.

He inhales, nodding. "Fair enough."

"Then what?" I ask.

"We go and we get your father back." He doesn't add his daughter. I think he knows that she's likely gone by now. Whatever they do with the girls, they aren't the same. Whatever he finds of Dahlia, it won't be her anymore, just like Stacia's not Stacia anymore.

"Deal," I say. "We should also contact Detective Bowen."

"Yes. The question is, in what order?"

"Detective Bowen, Archives, Forest." Even just saying it makes my stomach churn.

"Gotcha. Okay." He sniffs, then finishes his toast, then drinks down the rest of his coffee. He wipes his hands on his jeans and stands up. "I'm going to go home and shower. I'll text you when I'm on my way back."

I trail after him. We both pause at the door. Our eyes meet. I want to tell him how grateful I am he's helping me. That I'm not alone. He gives me a crooked smile, his eyes softening. We're allies, nothing more, nothing less.

"I'll be back soon. Will you be all right?" he asks.

"Yes."

Still, I watch him walk down to the sidewalk before locking the door, turning back to the now-empty house. I remember the odd figure I saw yesterday, and wonder what it was, if I imagined it. Parts of me that were asleep for so long are waking up. I feel jangly. Strung out. Reaching into my pocket, I take out the hag stone. It feels warm against my skin.

My heart racing, I recall Stacia, peering through it at the woods. Laughing. I wonder what she saw. What she knew, and I didn't.

Raising it to my eye, I look out of the front window, at the woods. I think I catch a sudden movement, but I blink, and it's gone. For a moment, I could have sworn it was wearing a hood.

CHAPTER EIGHTEEN

2000

STACIA AND I ARE BOTH STANDING OUTside of the cottage. The sun shines down on us through the branches. I close my eyes, tilting my face upwards like a sunflower. I listen to the sounds of the cicadas. A soft whispering—susurrations like wings.

When I open my eyes, I cannot see the source of the noise. I glance over at Stacia, who smiles at me.

"I feel… different," I say, placing my hands on my stomach. There's light, emanating from me, from Stacia. Power.

"Me too," she murmurs, closing her eyes and raising her face to the light.

"Like the sun is sitting in my belly." It's a curious feeling, one that makes me feel more powerful than I ever imagined possible. I'm just a girl. Human. Though my father has always encouraged me to follow my dreams, the world expects very little of me. Certainly nothing of this magnitude.

"You're Fenrir," she murmurs. "And I am Hela. Olive, we're like gods."

"Goddesses." Our eyes meet. She frowns at being corrected. It's there for a second, then gone in a flash. Her lips smile at me, though her eyes do not.

"Yes." There's an odd light in her eyes. Almost as if she's not quite there. Her fingers brush the hag stone around her neck. She holds out her other hand, and it seems to cup the sun as it slips beneath the trees. She sits up. "Come on."

We go into the cabin. We stay here a lot, after the blood oath. Telling our parents that we're at the other's house, we feast on junk food and stay up late into the night.

"No one is going to stop us," Stacia says, spinning in lazy circles. "Now, we can do more than just find lost children."

"What do you mean?" I lean back onto my pillow, taking a gulp of Coke, watching Stacia, lit up in the glow of the lantern. It's only now I realize we've not been looking for lost children. Not in weeks.

"We can do anything," Stacia says, kneeling. "Pierce the veil, get revenge on Horrorshow and Krissy..."

"How?" I can't deny consequences for their mean-spirited actions wouldn't be horrible. But I also don't want to harm anyone. I realize now Stacia was upset by Krissy's tribunal. She's never let on, holding the hurt inside of herself, and allowing it to fester.

She doesn't answer, just brings the hag stone up to her eye, looking at me through the hole. She smiles, as though she knows something I don't. I wonder what she sees. I don't ask, she doesn't say. Another lost opportunity. One of many that will haunt me over the years.

"Do you think that Old Witch Annabelle lived here?" I ask.

"I know she did." Her certainty gives me chills.

"How?" I sit bolt upright.

"She's still here. Can't you feel her?" She takes my hand. "Close your eyes, focus."

I close my eyes. The room is silent. Nothing moves. I feel nothing, and then, something—there's a cold ripple in the air behind me. Suddenly, I sense her—a presence weighing me down. I feel a cool breath on the back of my neck, causing all the hairs to rise.

A cold hand lands on my shoulder. I turn, finding myself face to face with Old Witch Annabelle. Deep wrinkles cut into her flesh. Her corpse blue lips droop downward. Her mouth drops open unnaturally wide as she screams. Limbs frozen, my heart hammers in my chest, and I watch as her eyes turn to black pits. She sucks all the light out of the air.

Scrabbling backward, I try to get away from her, but her long fingers are tangled in my hair. I can feel her despair. Her loss. Her grief, overwhelming me. Suddenly, Stacia laughs, and Old Witch Annabelle is gone, banished. In the light, I glare at her, feeling betrayed.

"You should see your face," she says, solemnly. It's as though nothing's happened.

"What was that?" I ask, still feeling the chill air from Old Witch Annabelle. My heartrate is still racing.

"A ghost." Stacia says it matter-of-factly. She shrugs and stands up. I'm staring at her. She seems… different. Rangier. More comfortable than usual.

"You believe in ghosts?"

"Don't you?"

I shrug. I didn't before. But I do now. I want to leave. I wonder if Annabelle has been here the whole time, watching us. There's an underlying menace to the place now, just like in a bad dream.

"She wants her daughter back," Stacia says. She turns towards the window. Her arms are folded as she looks out into the darkness.

"Can we help her?"

"No."

"Why not?"

"Because the Moon-Eyed Folk will never give her back."

"Who are the Moon-Eyed Folk?"

"You know them. You call them the Fae."

My mind goes to the figures, standing silently among the trees. I want to ask her who this is. I want to know more. But I'm shaken by what's just happened. Before, this place felt like it was ours—a sanctuary. But the cabin has never been ours. It's Annabelle's.

Danger seeps in at the edges. I look over at the locket one last time. I want to leave, so I pick up my backpack, sling it on. I begin to walk back, tears stinging my eyes, causing my vision to blur. I feel betrayed by Stacia for laughing at me. For making me feel small.

"Olive?" Stacia calls out. "Where are you going?"

I do not answer, tears spilling down my cheeks. I can't forgive her, so I keep walking. Stacia doesn't follow me. Somehow, that makes it worse. It's like she doesn't care she's hurt me. After this, my best friend is like a stranger to me.

CHAPTER NINETEEN

2003

IT'S BEEN ALMOST THREE YEARS SINCE Stacia's disappearance. It's the first night of the special exhibit at the Blackwell Historical Society. Dad's really excited. I don't leave the house often. Not for anything social, at least. But this is really important to Dad, and so I've put on my best dress—it's black. I wore it to my grandparents' funerals, as well as the memorial service for Stacia.

We're in his truck. He keeps tugging at his tie. The radio's turned up, playing Bruce Springsteen. Dad's tapping his fingers. If I close my eyes, it's like I'm little again. The wind ruffles my hair.

"I want you to see it," Dad says, as we pull into the parking lot, the wheels of his beat-up truck crunching in the stones. "Before everyone else does."

"Okay." I'm excited for my dad. I haven't looked forward to anything in a very long time. He's full of anxious but happy energy. Mostly, I'm just going through the motions.

The Historical Society is in a boxy, red brick building, which used to be the home of one of Blackwell's founders—Jonathan Forrester Millhouse and his wife, Elizabeth, and their brood of ten children. Jonathan and Elizabeth lost all of them but one before adulthood. It's said Jonathan was cursed by Old Witch Annabelle.

We go inside—there are a few people setting up the refreshment tables. Dad's boss, Eudora Millhouse, is there—a slender, elegant woman, with pure white hair she wears in a bun. She's the direct ancestor of Jonathan and Elizabeth. As such, she's head of the Millhouse Trust, which is money held to keep the Archives alive and well.

"Olive," she says. "Welcome. It's been a long while since you've been here."

"Ms. Millhouse," I reply. She takes my hand in both of hers. They're warm, soft from the expensive, rose hand lotion she always uses. When I was small, she would allow me to take some from the little jar she keeps in her desk.

"It's good to see you," she says. "Has your father mentioned we're looking for a summer intern?" I glance over at Dad, raising an eyebrow.

"I was planning on it," he replies. I have the feeling the two of them have already decided I'm going to do it. I'm okay with this. Excitement at the prospect fills me, for the first time in a long while.

Ms. Millhouse winks at me. "Enjoy the exhibit," she says. "It's very interesting. Congratulations, Merrick." She smiles at Dad, placing her hand on his lower arm.

"Thank you." He places a hand on my shoulder, ferrying me gently towards the door. Together, we slip inside. He speaks in a low voice. "You don't have to if you don't want to."

"I think I might," I tell him. It would be a change of pace—instead of sitting at the house, drowning myself in paperbacks from the library and chocolate ice cream. I'm a teenage girl with no friends—I need something different to do.

The door shuts softly behind us, and Dad flicks the light switch. The room has been transformed. I stand and allow myself a moment to absorb it. There are several different display cases with different yellowed documents inside them under bright lights. There are maps of the Deeping Woods, and of Blackwell.

There are also sketches, artist renderings of what look like pale aliens. They are round headed, with no hair, their limbs slender. They have large, black eyes. My stomach does an odd, roiling flip. I swallow back the bile that rises in my throat.

"So," he says. "This is it."

"Are those aliens?" I ask, walking over to the pictures of the pale, little people. My heart is racing.

"The Native Americans called them the Moon-Eyed Folk," he replies. "Apparently, they were here, in the lower part of Appalachia. The Cherokee chased them out of the area. No one ever heard from them again."

"Where did they go?" The story makes me sad. A lot of things make me sad these days, so I don't tell my father this.

"The only place where they'd be safe," he says, pointing to the maps of the cave systems. "They went underground."

"Really?" I shiver.

"Yes. There's a cave system that travels all the way through the Appalachians. There are myths and legends about cave-dwelling people throughout all of history. Some people believe they're Fae."

I look over at him sharply, but he's still looking at the map. My heart's pounding, hard. The sound of it is loud in my ears. "Is that why people disappear in the Deeping Woods?" I ask, my mouth utterly dry.

"It might very well be," he says, frowning. He coughs, clearing his throat. "It's just—just a theory." He looks at me. The sad look he gets whenever we almost talk about Stacia.

"By who?" I ask, balling my hands into fists.

"Paranormal enthusiasts," he replies. "I guess—well, I guess I was trying to see if the historical evidence added up."

"Does it?"

He sniffs, wrinkling his nose. He's gone into academic mode. He's not noticing my panic. "It does, a little."

I want to ask him more, but then the doors open, and Ms. Millhouse peers inside. My father and I both turn towards her.

"Merrick?" she asks, with a small smile. "Are you ready?"

"Go get 'em, Dad," I say, hiding the overwhelming feelings I'm having. When I glance to my left, I see a display case. Inside are several cloth poppets, just like the ones I found in the cabin. They are yellow with age. Quickly, I turn away from them.

Dad beams at me, adjusting his tie. "Thanks, kiddo." He pats me on the shoulder.

I want to look at the data on my own—to add my conclusions to it. I linger, while Dad goes to the doors—I can see the crowd of people who have shown up.

I find myself looking at a leather-bound diary in one of the glass cases. The plaque reads it belonged to a woman who was accused of killing her daughter, Viola. Annabelle Parker. Old Witch Annabelle. As I read it, something stirs in the back of my mind. It's there for a second, then it's gone.

∾

"HERE, behind these doors, is an exhibit showing the line where myth and fact are one. Perhaps, myths aren't so much stories, but facts which seem incredible. Perhaps, what was once known to be truth becomes a story. I think that magic is something that we traded for a magic of a different kind," Dad says. I am standing off to the side. The turnout is impressive, and there's a low hum of voices as he speaks.

"Here at the Archives, we have hard evidence of these myths. In Blackwell's history, we have had strange disappearances, ones which have repeated themselves. I think it lies in the old Cherokee myths of the Moon-Eyed Folk—a race of beings with pale skin and eyes which couldn't see in sunlight—and the black stone well which gives this town its name."

"What are you talking about, Merrick?" a voice says from the back of the crowd.

Dad laughs. "I beg you, please leave your preconceived notions of what is real and unreal at the door. I've gathered facts that can be found here in the archives. Proof, if you will. So, please, come in with an open mind, and allow your notions to be challenged."

There's scattered clapping as everyone begins to speak excitedly. My heart's racing at what my father has let slip—Stacia was not the first person in the history of Blackwell to disappear into the woods. Dad comes to stand beside me. His arms are crossed, and he's tapping his foot. Nerves.

We stand off to the side, watching all the people coming inside. Ms. Millhouse comes to stand with us.

"Nice intro, Merrick," she says.

"Thank you, Eudora."

The people continue to talk in low voices, but my attention is wandering. I watch all of them, milling around in the room. I note that Horrorshow and Johnny are laughing, standing beside the picture of the Moon-Eyed People. Everyone's all talking amongst each other. It's like being in the center of a beehive.

"Aliens! Ha!" a man says, drawing me out of my thoughts. I glance over at my father in time to watch his smile fade.

"What are you trying to do here, Merrick?" one person asks.

"Do the Kessels know about this?" another person adds, angrily. My stomach does a nervous flip.

"Are they angry that you're attributing their daughter's disappearance to alien cave dwellers?"

I watch as Dad's face falls. Ms. Millhouse immediately goes into damage control mode.

"Listen," she says. "Merrick has found ample proof in the archives to support these claims. If you would all take a moment to look at this empirically..."

I reach out, taking Dad's hand, squeezing it. I wait until he looks at me. I know how hard he's worked on this—how excited he's been to finally share his work. In this moment, I feel love for him. He's really tried hard. All these months of me trying to find some kind of normal, and he's just wanted to help. This was what he did. It was for me, to help me figure out what happened to me that night, what happened to my friend.

He finally looks at me. His eyes are watery behind his glasses.

"There are more things in Heaven and Earth than are dreamed of in your philosophies, Horatio," I say, giving him a small smile.

Dad smiles, squeezing back. "Thanks, Olive."

"Stacia and I believed in these sorts of things," I say, wishing desperately she was here right now. "She would have loved this." I know this to be true. These are the sorts of answers she would have gobbled up, faster than her favorite candy bars.

"Well, it wasn't the reaction I'd hoped for, but at least people showed up." He shrugs.

"True. I think we could use some ice cream," I tell him. "To celebrate your hard work."

He beams at me, even though there's a sadness there, too. One which has been around since my mother left.

"You can tell me all about the Moon-Eyed Folk," I say. I truly am interested because I've heard that term before. Perhaps he has some of the answers I've been looking for.

"People round these parts call them goblins," he says, with an empty laugh. "Though Annabelle Parker referred to them as children in her diary."

"Sounds about right," I tell him, recalling the picture. Something catches in my mind, an image of a small, hooded figure stepping out of the darkness in the woods. It's there for a second, then gone again. Together, we walked out of the Historical Society and into the purpling twilight outside.

Throughout the rest of the evening, while he eats his Rocky Road, he's trying to keep a brave face on for me. I eat my mint chip, keep up a steady stream of conversation. I want to take the hurt away from him, but don't know how.

It's the worst part of being a child—when you learn that you can't protect your parent. How can I? I'm still just a kid. He's an adult, learning how it is to find that your own ideas aren't respected.

Years later, I find he had kept digging. He has kept looking for the answers he knows I'll need. It's not until much, much later, I realize I should have asked him more about Annabelle Parker's diary.

CHAPTER TWENTY

2024

WHEN HARLEY RETURNS, I'M SITTING IN the kitchen sipping from a cup of coffee and staring at the beams of sunlight, pouring through the window. The way the dust motes float and gleam, they remind me of something, but what that is, I don't know.

I hear the door open. He hasn't knocked, just let himself in. I sit, listening to the soft thud of his heavy shoes on the carpet. He peers in, clearly expecting me. I smile, stretching my lips upward.

"You ready to go?" he asks. He's dressed in gray, tactical pants with lots of pockets. A black t-shirt. Hiking boots. A backpack.

"Almost." I sip my coffee, letting my eyes drift back to the sunlight. A memory, elusive—a flash of Stacia, her hair fanning out around her on the ground. Annabelle, her cold face. Dead eyes.

"What are you thinking about?" Harley asks.

"Annabelle Parker."

"Who?" He sits heavily down in the chair across from me.

"Old Witch Annabelle. Her name was Annabelle Parker," I reply, bringing my coffee cup to my lips. Harley's frowning, his eyes are intent. We're getting to the heart of the matter—the answers that we're both searching for.

"She lived in a secluded cabin in the woods. Her daughter Viola went missing, and she was blamed for it. She spent the rest of her life in prison." I squint. "Sound a little familiar? It was part of my dad's exhibit."

"Wait. Old Witch Annabelle lost her daughter, too?" he asks. I can see what he's thinking—he and Annabelle had something in common.

It registers—Dad left this out of his explanation. I look at him in surprise. "Yes, Harley. Her diary was what originally inspired my Dad to make that exhibit." I shake my head. I've not thought about Old Witch Annabelle in years. Now, I know she's an integral part of the puzzle.

"Where is it?" he asks, clearly coming to the same conclusion.

"If I had to guess, his desk at the Archives." I don't believe he'd bring it home. Not when anyone might take it.

"Is that why you want to go there?" he wonders.

"Yes. I read the diary during one of the summers that I worked there."

"What did it say?"

"I can't remember well. You know, I'm pretty sure that Stacia and I used to hang out at her cabin." I'm beginning to put things together—things which I must have known, deep down inside of myself.

"Really?" He's looking at me with respect.

"Yes. We found a locket there, with a young woman and a baby's pictures in it. I think it was them." I shake off the eerie feeling that I have—that things are coming together, events repeating. "Come on. Let's get going. We've got a long day ahead of us."

We walk the few blocks to the police station in complete silence, both of us lost in our thoughts. We both stop outside. We haven't considered how we're going to approach Johnny. I'm a bit nervous, because I don't know what to say.

"What's the plan?" I ask him, wiping my sweaty palms on my pants. I'm dressed for hiking, in yoga pants and a t-shirt, my running shoes.

"We go in, and we ask." He seems much too confident this is going to work. He's standing with his hands on his hips.

"Are you sure this is the best way to approach him?" I ask, doubtfully.

"He wouldn't appreciate it if we made him meet us out in the woods," he says. "If he's going to help us, then he'll let us just walk into evidence." This seems too good to be true.

"You mean you don't want to meet him in the woods," I mutter. Even I don't want to enter the woods. But that's beside the point. Cold washes over me. I would feel so much better going in if we had Johnny with us.

"As much as I'd like to believe in authority figures, Olive, they've all failed me in the past." He smiles at me. "I was hoping one of us could distract him, while the other gets into evidence."

I roll my eyes, to cover the sinking feeling I have inside. "Why am I not surprised? I don't want to do anything illegal, Harley."

"You distract him. Get him to give you details. You are distraught, aren't you?" he asks.

"That's a leading statement," I remark, "have you done this before?"

"Something… like it." He beams devilishly.

I should have known. A thought accompanied by another sinking feeling. "Hold up. If we're truly on the same side, then you need to tell me *before* we are walking into the police station that we're going to be breaking the law." I stop walking at the stairs. He doesn't.

"You're right. I'm sorry. We'd best get a move on, though." He strides through the doors in front of me, and I hustle to catch up.

There's no one at the front desk. Harley leans over it, slamming his hand repeatedly down on the bell to get someone's attention.

"Hello?" I call out. "Detective Bowen?"

He peers around the corner, smiling as he sees me. He has a folder in his hand, he closes it quickly.

"Miss Sanderson. To what do I owe the pleasure?" This is when he sees Harley, leaning over the counter, and his smile falters then crashes into a positively dark, wary look.

"I was wondering if you have any updates?" I ask quickly. "On my father?"

He sighs. "No. We searched along the Snake River, looked around. There was no sign of anyone having been there recently. As a matter of fact, most of the fishing spots have been closed."

"Why?" I ask, furrowing my brows. It's the middle of summer. Not to mention, the weather's been perfect.

"Algae Bloom." His face is closed off, and I know it's because Harley's here. I just don't know why. Harley hasn't told me everything.

"Ah. Have you checked any of the mine shafts?" I ask, going over possible places my father might have gone. "Any of the caves?"

"Ah, yes. A few of them, although there were no recent signs of any human entry." He's studiously avoiding Harley with his gaze. Suddenly, I realize I should have come here alone. These two men are no longer friends. The icy silence between them is suddenly obvious.

"Johnny," Harley says, cutting in. I watch as the detective rearranges his features. Something happened between them. I wonder what it is, and my gut tells me it's about Dahlia McCallis. "Olive and I are doing our own investigation, so we're going to need to see the items that you took from Merrick's house."

He just lays it all out there. I give him props. He got right to the point. I've sucked the insides of my cheeks in, and I'm biting down. The iron taste of blood accompanies it. I've been trying so hard to keep it all together—for my father. It feels like I've gotten nowhere. The insides of my cheeks are raw.

"This is an active investigation, Harley," Johnny says tiredly. "You of all people should not be meddling in it. Whoever it is behind it, is dangerous. They've been taking kids for a long time. Mr. Sanderson might have gotten in their way."

I perk up, listening closely. This is telling. They think my father was taken. By a person. *A dangerous person*, I think, my stomach flipping over queasily. I bite back the words, *may not have been a person.*

"Well, if you had looked into every avenue twelve years ago, then we wouldn't be here today," Harley shoots back.

Johnny's face crumples. "How can you say that? I have spent years looking for Dahlia."

"Then why haven't you found her?" Harley demands.

"I don't know," Johnny whispers. His face crumples in on itself. When he says it, I believe him. He's struggling because he's afraid to admit it's paranormal. Johnny Bowen, small-town detective, is frightened... just like I am. Just like Harley is.

"It's because you're looking for a person," Harley goes on.

"Harley..." Johnny looks even more concerned than he did before. I can see this isn't going the way that Harley meant it to—nor will it.

"No. There's something out there, in those woods. If you aren't looking for it, then you're never going to find it," Harley is raging. He's like a stick of dynamite, already lit and being thrown through a plate glass window. I need to stop him before he blows everything sky-high.

"Harley," I begin, trying to get him to lay off. He's pushing Johnny too hard and too far. We're losing him. We need his help.

"What are you talking about?" Johnny asks.

"The paranormal, Johnny," Harley snaps.

"Harley..." His brow is creased. He looks at me. "Are you part of this insanity, too, Olive?"

"It's not insanity. It's the truth," Harley announces before I can get a word in. "You can either help us, or you can step out of our way." I'm standing there, my mouth open, ready to respond.

He rubs his chin. "Well, I can't help you," he says. "I just... it's impossible. Do you hear yourself? You sound insane."

"It believes in you, no matter what you think of it," Harley tells him. "If you don't start believing in it, then you might be next... Mae might be next."

Johnny sighs sadly. Harley glares back at him. I can feel his anger, radiating off him. Harley exhales sharply, throwing his hands in the air. "Okay. Well, you think on it. Let us know. Come on, Olive. He's not going to help us." Harley turns and stalks out of the precinct. Johnny follows us towards the door.

As we're crossing the lobby, the door bursts open and Krissy enters. She's pale, clearly shaken. The three of us stop. She looks a wreck—she's in a sweatshirt and a pair of joggers, the knees green. Her hair is rumpled, dark splotches of mascara running down her cheeks.

"Krissy?" Harley asks. "What's the matter?"

"My daughter's missing," she says, causing my stomach to drop. Harley and I share a glance. When I look at Johnny, he's gone an odd shade of green.

It's happened again. My father was not the target—Ada was.

"Tell us," Harley says to Krissy, who has just burst into a fresh round of tears. My heart goes out to her.

"No," Johnny says. "Don't—"

"We were taking a walk by the woods, down by the creek," Krissy blurts out. "I was distracted for a second. I just looked away for a moment to look up at an egret. It startled me. It was so big. One second, she was there, the next, she'd vanished."

"I'll take this from here," Johnny says, getting in between us. "The two of you should go home. Wait for news." He's glaring at us sternly.

"All right," Harley says, holding his hands up. Johnny spears him with a look that throws daggers. We both watch as he places a hand on Krissy's shoulder and guides her into an office. We are to go home, wait for news. As we both walk out together, I know—we're the only people who are going to be able to do anything.

CHAPTER TWENTY-ONE

2024

WE'RE SILENT AS WE WALK THROUGH the parking lot. My heart is pounding in my chest. The constant thump-thump as it ticks away towards the end of my life. I can't shake the feeling that soon, I will run out of time. I'm reaching the conclusion.

"He'll come around," I say. I know this for certain. Johnny will realize he needs us.

"Yeah. He'll have to," Harley mutters, inhaling as he wipes at his eyes. "Especially once he starts looking at the evidence."

"Are you okay?" I ask him. He looks grayer than usual.

"No. We should get going. The Archives close soon." I follow him down the block. He's walking quickly, and I jog to keep up with him.

"What happened?" I ask him.

"What do you mean?" He keeps his gaze on the street, watching all those who are going about their lives, none the wiser. Do they know? Do they know there's something in those woods, just over there?

"You used to be best friends," I prompt Harley.

"It's just what happens," he says. "People grow apart."

"Is it?" I don't know if Stacia and I would have grown apart. I never got the chance to know, though I'd have loved to have been given the option. We got in a fight, but I've always believed we would have figured it out.

He stops. He seems to shrink down in size. "If Stacia told you the Fae had taken her, would you believe her? Even if you'd never seen them?"

"Yes." I don't hesitate. I always believed her.

"Johnny won't believe me," he says. "He won't believe a word I say. No one will."

"I do."

"Yeah. You and Merrick." He gives me a lop-sided grin. His eyes have a haunted cast to them. He knows this isn't going to end well. But he's still moving forward. We both are.

"Let's get going," I say. I haven't been to the Archives in years. They look the same as they have for as long as I can recall. I imagine that they haven't changed since the Millhouse family stopped using it as their ancestral palace. When the door opens, it even smells the same—old papers, leather, and dust.

Eudora Millhouse smiles when she looks up to see me. She's gotten older—her hair's now pure white, though her skin is flawless. She still wears the same shade of lipstick.

"Olive," she says, standing up from her desk. She walks over to me, placing the glasses dangling from a beaded chain onto her nose. She's smaller than I remember. "How are you holding up?" She's keeping her face from crinkling with sorrow. There's a painful lump in the back of my throat.

"I'm trying to do what I can," I say, taking her small, bony hand in mine. Her skin is warm and soft. When I look into her eyes, they're watery. "I should have come here sooner."

"We are all thinking of Merrick," she says, meaning the small handful of people who dwell among the town archives. Mostly local researchers, historians. Some professors.

"When was the last time you saw him?" I ask, folding my hands in front of me. For once, Harley is letting me take the lead, and I'm grateful to him for it.

"He came into work," she says. "He stayed the whole day, then left on time. The next day, he never showed up. When I called his phone, he didn't answer, so I called the police."

I nod, biting my lip. This is all out of character for Dad, who never missed a day of work in his life. "Would it be all right if we checked his office?"

"Of course. The police took a look, but didn't find anything, but maybe you'll see something they didn't," she says.

We all walk down the hall. Harley trails behind me and Ms. Millhouse. "What was he working on?" I ask.

"He was still working on the Annabelle Parker case. He was writing his book, of course. Though, I imagine he told you all about it."

"That's the problem, Eudora," I say. "He didn't."

She looks at me, blinking owlishly. Worry lines her face. "That is concerning," she says in a low voice. She turns the key in the lock, opening the door. "Well, let me know if there's anything that I can do to help." She looks me in the eye. "This place isn't the same without Merrick. Too quiet. I'd do anything to get him back here."

"Where he belongs," I murmur.

"Exactly so," she says. "I'll be in my office." She walks down the hallway, the sound of her soft-soled shoes padding gently as she walks.

I enter the room. Natural sunlight spills through the blinds onto the honey wood of Dad's desk. The bookshelves are stuffed. Piles of papers and notebooks cover the desk. I sit down in his chair, listening to the familiar creak of the leather.

I exhale, forcing the tears back. I've never been here without Dad popping in and out periodically. This is his space. It seems empty without his booming, sunny presence. Too quiet, as Eudora pointed out. I swallow, then I slide open the drawer, my stomach sinking.

"What?" Harley asks. "What is it?"

"The diary's not here," I say, looking at the familiar contents. It's the only thing missing. Instead, a copy of the children's cookbook my dad and

I used while I was growing up is placed inside. My hands shaking, I pick it up, sobbing.

I open to the page on homemade tomato soup, our favorite recipe, paired with grilled cheese. Taped to that page, there's an envelope. My name is written in my father's familiar handwriting.

CHAPTER TWENTY-TWO

2003

DAD AND I DRIVE TO THE ARCHIVES together. It's the first day of my internship. Though it's walking distance, we pile into his truck. Ms. Millhouse is already there when we arrive.

"I've put on a pot of tea," she says. "Help yourselves."

"Lovely. Thank you, Eudora," Dad replies.

"It's good to have you here, Olive. Your dad's been excited to show you around." She gives me a conspiratorial wink as she pours out the tea into several paper cups.

I smile, curving my lips upward. I'm no longer used to smiling. It's foreign. "Thanks." I glance at Dad. He's running his fingers through his hair.

"Come on," he says, handing me a paper cup of hot tea. I take it, then follow him to his office. "I—I thought you'd be interested in this." He gestures to a book that sits out on his desk.

"What is it?" I ask, sitting down in the comfy, green chair tucked into the corner of the office.

"The diary of Annabelle Parker," he says, placing the leatherbound book in front of me. He sits in his chair, which creaks loudly as he settles down into it. As I run my hand over the leather, I get a thrill running up my arms. "I know you and Stacia went into the woods."

My head snaps up. I arrange my features, so I'm giving nothing away. Luckily, Dad hasn't noticed. He's facing the window as he opens the blinds.

"I think you might find answers in there about the town," he tells me. "Annabelle Parker was much like you. She loved the woods, too."

"Tell me more about her." I take a sip of my tea. It's hot, sweet.

He nods, rubbing his whiskery chin. "From what I've read, she was smart. She was a strong believer in the Fae."

My heart just about stops. Over the past months, I've come to the realization Stacia must have gone with those strange, hooded figures in the woods. My blood is electric with terror.

"She was a wise woman, learned. People in the town would come to her to treat different ailments. She worked, secretly, as a midwife. She—ah—helped women who found themselves pregnant." He goes a little pink in the face.

I nod.

"She lived there with her daughter, Viola," he goes on.

"What happened to her husband?" I ask.

"She was never married, and she never mentions him. It was rumored, in the town, that Viola's father was the Devil himself."

"So they thought her a witch?"

"From what she says in her diary, she *was* a witch," he tells me. We both share a look. He knows, I think to myself. He knows everything.

"What happened to her?" My mouth is dry, even though I've been drinking tea.

"She died in jail," he replies. "She never told anyone where she buried the body. She claimed she was innocent."

"They had no idea?" I ask, though I think: *Viola wasn't dead. There was never a body to find.*

"No. They all believed that she'd killed her daughter in some sort of a Satanic ritual. The villagers tried to set her cabin on fire."

"Can I read it?" I ask, more curious than ever.

He hands me the diary, and a pair of the special cotton gloves they have you wear. I slip my hands into them.

"I'll be in the stacks," Dad tells me.

"Okay."

He pauses by the door. "It's good to have you here, Olive."

"Thanks Dad. It's good to be here." I'm surprised to find I mean it. For the first time in a long time, I'm excited to be alive. We share a smile.

He leaves, and I open the book. That familiar thrill of magic flashes across my palms, even through the gloves. What's immediately clear to me is this: It's not a diary. It's a grimoire.

Spell-booke of Annabelle Parker

I flip to the back, and I notice the back endpapers are peeling upward. I gently prise upward with a letter opener from Dad's desk. There's a small, brown piece of paper, folded neatly underneath.

They came in the night as they always do. Their skin is too delicate for the sun. It's pale, glossy—fish white. They wanted to know what I would give, in exchange for my daughter.

I said, nothing. She's all I have.

The Fae Folk are cruel gods. Twelve years ago, they gave her to me, and now, they want to take her back.

I continue reading—my tea goes cold on the desk beside me. By the end of it, I think I know what it is. But I don't know how I will get Stacia back from them. I don't have anything to trade for her.

CHAPTER TWENTY-THREE

2024

WAVES OF COLD AND HOT WASH OVER me. There's a ringing in my ears, like an alarm bell, as I tear the envelope open, unfold the letter inside. My hands are shaking as I read:

Dear Olive,

I knew that you would come here, looking for answers. Annabelle Parker's diary was only the beginning. She was a lonely person— most of those in Blackwell would stay away from her, whispering of witchcraft and dark alchemy.

Annabelle made contact with those who live in the woods. She asked them for help conceiving a daughter, and they helped her— or so she claimed in the diary. Twelve years later, Viola Parker went missing.

Annabelle Parker was convicted of her daughter's murder, though Viola's body was never found. Annabelle remained in jail until her death. Though many in this town know her name— Old Witch Annabelle, they have forgotten her story. They have forgotten those who live in the woods.

Even though every twelve years, at least one girl from Blackwell goes missing. Viola Parker, Stacia Kessel, Dahlia McCallis— they are part of a pattern that is nearly two hundred years old. Perhaps even older, though I cannot find the records to substantiate it. I started on this path to find answers— to free you, Olive. From the darkness that has been following you for twenty-four years. If I am missing, then I must beg you— do not come looking for me. It is already too late.

You cannot fight those who live in the woods— they take what pleases them, and they keep it forever. I have put the diary someplace safe— somewhere that they cannot enter.

I love you. I would not have traded our time together for the world, even though we haven't been as close as we once were. Please understand— I can't risk you following me into danger.

All my love,

Dad

There's still a ringing in my ears, and my stomach is turning nauseously. I feel a tear rolling down my cheek. I look out the window. From here, I can see the woods. Birds rise from the trees. I watch the arcane shapes they make.

"Olive?" Harley murmurs. Without looking at him, I hand him the letter.

∾

HARLEY and I walk back down the hall in defeated silence. The diary was our one lead, and it's not even here. Who knows where he might have put it? My Dad's letter has only brought up more questions, rather than answers. I should have expected this, yet I'm truly disappointed.

Ms. Millhouse peers out of her office as we walk by. "Did you find anything?" she asks.

"No," I say, shaking my head. "Thanks for letting us look, though."

"Of course, Olive. I hope they find him soon. This place won't be the same without Merrick."

"No," I agree. "It won't." A sharp pain twinges in my chest. My head is spinning. My throat is tensed, painfully, as I try not to dissolve into tears again.

She places a hand on my arm, squeezes it. "Let me know if you need me. I'm old, but my mind is good."

I nod, smiling, though my eyes blur with tears. I'm confused, and even more scared than I was. Harley places a hand on my other arm, then guides me outside.

We walk out and into the sunlight. I stand there, blinking. The world seems to spin like a top. I don't know what to do. Where to go. I look down at the letter in my hand.

"Come on," Harley says. "Let's get something to eat."

Harley just walks beside me as we go to the diner. Sitting down, I order a hamburger with fries. Harley orders the same.

"What date is that?" Harley asks, pointing to something Dad scrawled at the bottom: 10/07/2000.

"The day Stacia went missing," I whisper, reaching up to wipe at my cheeks.

He nods. "How are you holding up, partner?" When I look up, he's watching me with concern, and understanding. He's been where I am—when he lost Dahlia. I can talk to him.

"I feel like we're running out of time," I say. "That we're never going to get him back. He's all that I have." I unfold the sheet of paper, pressing it flat. *Those who live in the woods.*

"Can I see that?" he asks, holding out a hand.

I slide it over to him, watching his face as he reads it. The food comes, and I dig in. It's odd, sitting here quietly with him. I order coffee, he continues to stare at it. He's tapping his fingers on the table, a steady drumming, like rain.

"Someplace safe. Someplace they can't enter. Can you take me there?" he asks, finally looking up. "To the cabin?" Icy fear pours down my spine, but I nod. I can see his logic. After they took her daughter, Annabelle would have made sure her home was safe.

"Is there any way around it?" My stomach lurches, and I stop chewing.

"We have to go into the woods. You know that we have to." He takes my hand, and I almost flinch. He's right. I've known, ever since I got the call Dad had gone missing. After a moment, I grip his hand back. When I look into his eyes, I see my own despair reflected at me. "For Merrick," he whispers.

"And Stacia and Dahlia."

"Ada, too."

We both nod. I let go of his hand first. I feel… I don't know. There's no time to really dissect this strange relationship that's been born out of shared loss. In another life, I would have never seen him again. Never thought to trust him. I eat my food, drink my coffee. It should have a flavor, but it doesn't. Fear makes it taste like dust in my mouth. Out of my peripheral vision, I can see he's watching me eat. I look up at him, still chewing.

"What?" I ask.

"You eat like a dude." He quirks his eyebrow.

"Is that a compliment, McCallis?"

"Could be."

"Look, if I'm going to die today, then I want to do it on a full stomach," I mutter, taking another bite. Suddenly, it occurs to me: I'm going to die today. I look over at Harley, sitting across from me. He's thinking the same thing.

I'm hit with an overwhelming sense of déjà vu, to the point where I put my sandwich down.

"Olive?" Harley asks, his voice fading away.

I feel myself drift, into the distant past, as I realize…

CHAPTER TWENTY-FOUR

2000

...THIS IS THE EXACT SAME TABLE STACIA and I sat at, arguing about going back. Neither of us ate our food. When I look up, she's sitting across from me. She had cornered me, here. My book lies on the table, face down. She's waiting for me to speak, twirling her hair between two fingers. There's a smudge of dirt on her face. I look down at my still-full breakfast platter. There's a lump in my throat, as I try not to cry again.

"I don't want to go back," I tell her.

"What do you mean?" Her brow furrows deeply.

"You laughed at me," I said, hot tears prickling at the backs of my lids, blurring her features.

She sighs, toying with the straw in her chocolate milkshake. "It wasn't anything personal."

I swallow around the lump in my throat. "It was. How long did you know about her?"

She shrugs, still not looking at me. "She's always been there."

I sniffle. "She feels dangerous."

"She's harmless."

"I don't believe you," I say. "What else aren't you telling me?"

There's a long moment of silence as she thinks. I watch as her fingers brush the hag stone at her throat. She finally looks at me, smiling crookedly. "You'll figure it out." She might as well have slapped me.

"That's not good enough. You're supposed to be my friend." When she doesn't say anything, I get up, then storm out. I hear her calling for me, but she doesn't catch up with me. Tears streak down my cheeks as I go home. Alone.

I spent the last few days of summer break alone in my room. I re-read *The Oak Mage*, wishing that I was powerful, like Lady Morgana. After that, we returned to school. I'd see her in the hallways. She was suddenly dirty, her nails rimmed in dark dirt. Her hair was knotty, clotted with dry leaves. One day, she came to school in her white nightgown from the night of our blood oath.

Whenever she'd try to catch my eye, I turned away. If she wasn't going to apologize to me, then I didn't want anything to do with her. Not after she'd laughed at me. Not after she'd been keeping things from me. I don't know the exact day she stopped coming to school. However, I was the one called into the office. It was late September by then. I hadn't spoken to Stacia in almost a whole month.

When I entered the room, my stomach sank. Stacia's parents were there with the principal. And my dad. He breathed out a sigh of relief.

"What is it?" I ask, sinking down into the empty chair. My legs feel weak, shaky. I've never been in trouble before.

"Stacia hasn't been in school all week," the principal says, gently. "Her parents say that she hasn't come home, either. That she told them she's been staying with you."

I can feel everyone's eyes on me. I shake my head, swallowing. "We got in a fight," I say.

"Do you know where she would go?" Mrs. Kessel's voice is gentle. She doesn't believe that it's my fault, which makes all this worse.

Even though I'm still mad at Stacia, I don't want to get her in any more trouble than she already is. I can't tell them about the cabin. I can't tell them… anything, really. I decide to go on my own after school. I shake my head, no. Tears blur my vision, then fall down my cheeks making hot trails. I wipe at my eyes.

"I'm sorry," I say, sniffling. Dad comes over, placing a hand on my shoulder. "I don't know."

"Is there anything else?" he asks. "Is there… anything we can do to help?"

Mrs. Kessel is starting to cry, too. "What happened?" she asks. "What is happening to our little girl? She was… normal just a few weeks ago. Just the other day, I caught her… eating dirt in the backyard."

I'm crying even harder because I can't tell her what I know. It would sound insane, and it would only bring up more questions than answers. I shake my head, making eye contact. Her eyes are the same color as Stacia's. Dark brown.

"I don't know. I wish I did."

She crosses the room, taking me in her arms. "It's not your fault." This is the worst thing she could say. I think of Stacia, dirty and grim, dark circles under her eyes. Trying to catch my eye in the hallway. She's in over her head, and now I know I'll find her in the woods. I have to go.

Since I'm so upset, Dad takes me home. We have lunch in the kitchen—grilled cheese with tomato soup. I know he's dying to ask me questions, but he doesn't.

"Do you need anything?" he asks. "Is there… anything I can do?"

"No." There's only one thing to be done, and I need to go alone.

"Okay. I'll be down in the basement. If you need anything, just yell." Code for he's going to work on his book. I nod. He squeezes my shoulder as he passes me. I wait until his footsteps vanish down the stairs. I pause, listening to the sound of his typewriter. Then, I slip silently from the house.

CHAPTER TWENTY-FIVE

2000

I'M WALKING ALONG THE CREEK WHEN I feel it. An overwhelming sense of malice. As I watch, something black and smooth slithers through the water. In the back of my mind, I recall the Kelpie—the day we first found the cabin. I see a floating patch of dark seaweed. A black, scaled horse head rising above the water. It blinks golden eyes at me. It gives me the shudders. I feel my feet step towards it.

Words move through my mind, in a language that feels familiar. Old, like blood and stone. Tendrils of seaweed are wrapped around it. It's both beautiful and terrible to see. My nostrils are filled with a murky, muddy smell.

I begin to reach out with my hand when something stops me. It bares spiny teeth, snorts angrily. In a blink, it's gone, leaving only bubbles in the water. I step back, away from the creek, my heart racing.

I almost died just now I think to myself. I don't know what stopped it. Something is eluding me. Something important. Quickly, I move on, a gust of warm autumn air, running its fingers through my hair. I try not to think about what I've just seen. Nor the hunger, the malice I felt emanating from it.

Stacia's sitting out in front of the cabin. When I arrive at the cottage, she's crouching in the dirt outside of it. She doesn't look up, and when I approach, I see she's eating mushrooms, along with the dirt that clings to them. Her mouth is ringed with black. My stomach flips. She smiles, baring her dirty, black teeth.

"Everyone's looking for you." My voice is thin, reedy. I'm horrified by how she looks—her olive-toned skin, oddly pale.

She looks up, shrugging. "You aren't."

"I came here, didn't I? Why are you eating those? Aren't they poisonous?"

"It's an acquired taste. I'm hungry for them. She makes me… eat them. Good for the blood." Her eyes go from far away to sharp. "Why do you care?"

"Shouldn't I? You're my only friend." I wonder who she's talking about—surely not Old Witch Annabelle?

"You won't even look at me—at school." She stands up, moving faster than I expect. She moves with predatory grace. I stand my ground. She smells like she hasn't showered in ages. Her teeth are mossy this close. Her eyes have a darker gleam. I stare her down, swallowing back nausea. "You swore an oath."

"So did you," I remind her.

"Blood sisters." She's too close. Angry, too.

"You were mean to me." I raise my chin, standing my ground.

She seems to deflate. Sags into herself. Tears form in her eyes, making them glossy. "I'm sorry. I just—everything's insane. This cabin. The people who live in the woods. The—the—*she*. It's all making me insane." She sounds like herself for the first time in a long time.

"What are we going to do?" I ask, relieved to finally have my friend back.

"We need to end this. We need to go and see what lives there. She owes us. She owes us our wishes. Then, it'll all be over." She seems so sure of herself.

"How?" I ask. The task seems impossible.

She puts her cold, dirty hand to my sternum. "The light inside of us. That's what keeps us safe."

"What if you're wrong?"

"What if I'm right?"

"What if you're not? What if they're *dangerous*?"

"Then why are we still alive now? They've had so many chances to hurt us, and they've done nothing, Olive."

I sigh heavily. I can feel that light, that power inside of me. But when I look at Stacia, she looks sick. I need to get her back home.

"We have to get going. Before they come and look for us."

My heart is telling me this isn't going to be what she thinks it is. I don't know the "they" that she's referring to. Our families? The police? Or those that live in the woods? "After this, we'll go home?" I ask instead.

"Yes."

"We won't come back here anymore?"

"No." Stacia is grinning widely. She takes my hand. There's a small pimple, next to the corner of her mouth. Her forehead and nose are covered in white heads. I wonder when she last showered. I just want to get her home, safe.

"You promise, Stacia?"

"I promise."

It's going to have to be enough. On one hand, we might be allowed wishes. We may be the chosen ones, like Stacia thinks. Or we may meet something we didn't foresee, like the kelpie. Letting go of my hand, she walks into the woods. Sighing heavily, I follow her into the dark woods. As we enter them, the sun begins to sink down beneath the horizon.

CHAPTER TWENTY-SIX

2024

"EARTH TO OLIVE," HARLEY IS SAYING from somewhere nearby, while snapping his fingers. I blink, looking across the table at him.

I focus on him. "I remember everything." I shudder. "It's all coming back now…"

"Everything?" he whispers, to my surprise.

"Almost," I say, running my finger over the table, feeling the greasy film across it. "Come on. We have to go back to talk to Eudora."

"What for?" he asks as he pulls a few bills out of his wallet and throws them down on the table.

"We need to know more about Annabelle Parker," I tell him. "And those who live in the woods. Eudora Millhouse is the one other person in Blackwell who'll know about it."

As soon as we enter the Archives, she waves us inside. She's brewed tea while we were gone, and hands us both steaming mugs.

"I knew you'd be back. Come, let's sit in my office." She opens the door. "Have a seat." The chairs are all old leather, they protest as Harley and I sit down. The walls are floor to ceiling shelves, and there's a new, sleek laptop closed on the top of her mahogany desk.

I'm too distraught to drink the cup she handed me. I am so close to the precipice, and I know it. I'm so close to finding out all the answers I've been missing for so long.

She settles into her desk chair, then smiles. "What can I help you with?"

"We keep coming across 'those that live in the woods,'" I explain. "We'll need to know all that you know about them. And all that you know about Annabelle Parker."

"I had a feeling that you would," she replies, lacing her fingers together before her. "Your father was the one who wanted to know more about them. From our research, they've been there almost as long as memory has. The First Peoples have always told a story about the Moon-Eyed Folk. After the Cherokee forced them from their lands, they came here. The tribes avoided them, called this land cursed. As for Annabelle Parker, what you need to know about is Viola Parker, her daughter."

"The one who went missing?" Harley asks.

"Yes. In her diary, Annabelle claimed she had asked the fairies for a daughter. That they gave Viola to her, though she was vague on the details." She frowns thoughtfully before taking a sip of her tea.

"The fairies?" I murmur.

"Yes. She said there were people, living in the woods. That they were 'fae,' and they lived under the hills, much like the Unseelie Court."

"What happened?" Harley wonders.

"She claimed that when Viola was twelve, they wanted her to return on Samhain, when the veil between worlds was thinnest. Annabelle and Viola had made an agreement, where Viola would escape them and return to Annabelle. However, she never came back. Annabelle tried to get her back, but they wouldn't let her back in. Then, the authorities stepped in when they noticed that Viola was gone."

"Did the police look in the woods?" I ask.

"Yes. They scoured them, but there was no trace of Viola anywhere. So, they assumed that Annabelle had killed her. As soon as they heard her story, they figured she'd gone mad. Particularly since they found out that she was an accomplished writer, under the pseudonym, Rowena Pennyworth. She wrote about fairies, you see. They figured that it was more of the same brand of fiction."

I gasp, almost knocking over my untouched tea.

"What's the matter?" Harley's forehead is furrowed in concern.

"I read her often when I was a child. I loved her books," I say. "She wrote *The Oak Mage*." Her books told Stacia and I everything we needed to know to deal with those in the woods.

"Your father loved Pennyworth's books. She's still very widely regarded, you know," Eudora adds. "Not many people know the truth about her life."

"Annabelle died in prison," I murmur because the story must come to an end. "Her cabin burned."

"Caught fire but didn't burn. A curious happenstance." She regards me. "It's those people in the woods that your father went after. He was so sure that they were there. I tried to convince him not to go."

"What did he say?" I have a lump in my throat because I already know the answer. When she looks up, I know she knows, too.

"That he had to go—he had to do it for you, to make sure that you were safe."

"We have to go into the woods." I cannot hide the dread in my tone. I look at Harley, who nods gravely.

"Do you know where you're going?" Eudora asks.

"Unfortunately, I do," I say. "We have to go and get him. It's been far too long, and the police are probably looking for Ada. A child is a priority. A sixty-seven-year-old man isn't."

"They're looking for Ada," Harley says grimly. "But in the wrong place."

"True." To save one, we'll have to save both, just like in *The Oak Mage*.

"Good luck," she says. I clasp her hands. "Call me when you find him."

"Thank you for your help."

"I only wish I could do more," she says.

Harley and I leave the Archives. The sun is shining brightly. It feels like the day has gone on for ages, but it's barely past noon. I pause, but he keeps walking.

"Where are you going?" I ask.

"We'll need weapons," he says. "Come on." I follow him down the road.

"From where?" There's no time to go shopping.

"Come on," he repeats.

He begins walking in long, purposeful strides to his parents' house. He pulls a key from his pocket, opening the trunk to the SUV that's parked in the driveway. It's beat-up, the tires muddy.

Inside is a sleek gun safe. He unlocks this, revealing an arsenal. I've never seen anything like it, and I panic, turning to check the street. It's the middle of the day, in the middle of the week, so it's practically deserted.

"Harley! What if someone sees?" I hiss under my breath. He looks at me doubtfully and laughs.

"We're in Kentucky." He hands me a shot gun. "We're heading into the woods. Clearly, we're going hunting."

"Don't you need a game license?"

He pulls one out of his back pocket, tucked into a laminated case. I have nothing left to say. He's clearly come prepared. He hands me a hunting knife and a shot gun. He begins to fill a duffle with guns and ammunition. My hands are shaking. Terror is ice in my veins. The one thing I've feared these past twenty years is about to happen. Harley seems as cool as cucumber water.

Harley slings the duffle over his shoulder, then shuts the car door with a slam. "Let's go," he says and begins to walk away. I find that my knees have locked. He gets a little way down the sidewalk before turning back. "What's the matter?" he asks. My stomach is roiling with nerves like a nest of snakes. "You're scared," he goes on, coming back. "I'm scared, too."

"The last time I went into those woods, I came back alone."

"Not this time," he says, taking my hand in his. "This time, we're coming back with your dad and Ada." His hand is rough, warm. I look down at it, nodding. I think of safe things—my apartment, coffee and pancakes, the way Harley's eyes are softening.

Quickly, I remove my hand from Harley's. I look into his eyes. "Let's go."

He gives me a strange look, but then turns and walks alongside me. It's less than a block, and then we're there. The woods, their overwhelming swell of green. I can't help it, I stop again. This time, Harley notices immediately.

"Olive?" he asks.

"It looks the same," I say. "All these years and it looks exactly the same. I'm the only one that's changed."

A part of me has missed it here, and I cannot say this aloud, or the woods will hear it and use it against me. I've wanted to come back. I know where we're supposed to go.

"This way," I tell him, walking towards the creek. I know it, as well as I know the map of veins on the back of my hand. The way to Annabelle Parker's cabin.

CHAPTER TWENTY-SEVEN

2024

TWO GIRLS WENT INTO THE WOODS. Only one came out. History is repeating itself, in a way. Two people go into the woods. Who will come out? I can't help but wonder. How lucky can one person be? I finger the hag stone in my pocket as Harley and I walk in tense silence.

I pause when we reach the clearing where Annabelle Parker's cabin is. My eyes take in the familiar sight of the charred walls, the creepers. It looks the same. The woods have taken over a little bit more than I recall, but it looks the same.

"Should we take a look?" Harley asks.

Pulling the hag stone from my pocket, I peer at the cabin through the hole. In the doorway, I see Annabelle Parker step out of the shadows. She's as blue as the last time I saw her. Her lips, cheeks rotting away. Her eyes are just black pits. Her knotty hair floats on the air like flames. I feel menace coming off her in waves. Her message is clear: stay out.

"No. There's nothing there," I say, putting the stone back in my pocket. "We go this way—to the cave."

I turn away quickly. Harley follows. We're both silent. Too silent. I'm too used to him filling the space with idle chatter.

"I'm sorry," I tell him.

"For what?" He looks at me curiously.

"That I can't give you more information. I don't know what we'll find in the caves. I don't know how useful I am to you."

"I've searched these woods for years," Harley says, rubbing his scruffy chin with his hand. "This is way farther than I ever got on my own, Olive."

"What?" I ask, surprised. After all, how hard can it be to find a tumble-down cabin?

"There's something different about you," he says. "Something only you can do. I have never been here."

I nod, sniffing. I have no idea what it is. I slip my hand into my pocket again, feeling the now-familiar warmth of the hag stone.

"There's no one I'd rather have with me right now," he assures me. "Not even Johnny."

"You might regret that. I'm not that good of a shot." What I don't tell him is that I've never shot a gun before in my life. My father was into fishing, not hunting. I'm holding it, but I don't have a damn clue how to use it.

That's when I see it. Reflexively, I place a hand on his arm, gripping a fistful of his shirt.

"What is it?" he asks.

"We're here," I say, pointing to the cave. Even from this distance, I can feel cold air emanating from its depths. I can smell wet dirt, stone. A chill runs down from the nape of my neck to the base of my spine. "They're going to try to kill us," I tell him with utter certainty.

"I'm not worried about that," he says. I can hear the fatigue in his voice.

"This is the way in," I tell him, going to the darkened entrance. We turn on the headlamps, and then pause.

"Are you ready?" Harley whispers.

"No. I'll never be ready. Let's go."

Inside, it's very quiet. Except for the sound of water, dripping in the distance. I can feel something watching us. I can feel something stirring beneath my skin. The light inside of me has been asleep for so long, I'd forgotten it was there.

It's circulating through my veins for the first time in two decades. Stirring like leaves in a breeze. It's like I've been asleep all this time. Now, I'm coming awake again.

We both stop walking. Silence, deep and watchful. Bare feet, running in the distance. An overwhelming feeling of malice and déjà vu.

"They're coming," I say.

WE enter the cave, Stacia leading the way. For years, this is the last thing I remember: watching her vanish into the darkness as I follow her inside. As soon as we go into the dark, everything feels wrong.

"I can't see anything," Stacia says from somewhere nearby.

"Neither can I… Stacia?" I ask, reaching out. My fingertips brush against her arm, her skin cool, covered in goosebumps.

"Olive!" she gasps, grabbing my hand, though I cannot see her.

There's the sound of bare feet, running towards us. The copper taste of fear is in my mouth, accompanied by the sudden, overwhelming realization that even if I could run, I won't be able to outrun *them*. Those that live in the caves.

We're grabbed, pulled apart, so that I'm forced to let go of her hand. In moments, I'm lifted and then carried forward, stumbling on unseen stones. All I see is the dark, yet I know I'm surrounded. My heart beats loud as a drum in my ears—I have never been this frightened before. I feel small, strong hands grabbing me. The skin is soft and moist—mucus membranes. They smell mossy—mushroomy. I scream as I am pulled down to the cold, wet stone.

"Let me go," I beg as they push me down, my cheek pressing to the dirt. Tears well in my eyes as my pulse races. I scream, dirt grinding against my teeth. Suddenly, I am lifted and carried off. My head rolls backward, bones in my neck cracking. I'm looking up but see nothing. I can hear Stacia, mumbling nearby. We are brought down under the ground. Fast.

"Put me down!" Stacia demands, repeatedly, while I just scream, wordlessly. We have walked right into a trap. I don't want to think about what might happen. The fact is, I just don't know. Here, in the endless darkness, I don't know what to expect.

I'm not sure how long or how far we have traveled. I don't think we've ever been down this far in the caves during all our adventures. But this is not an adventure, or even a fairy story. This is a horror story, a real one, of blood and bone.

We're not going to make it out. We're trapped. This grim realization feels like a door slamming shut with utter finality. It's like we've already been buried alive. It's so dark. So cold.

Suddenly, I'm dropped, hard onto the ground. Feeling in the darkness, my hands touching cool, damp stone. Stacia bumps into me. We kneel, side by side, breathing heavily, clutching each other's freezing hands.

Suddenly, amber light emanates from the walls. I squint as my eyes begin to adjust. The floor is scattered with bones. My eyes fall upon a pile of small human skulls. There is a rib bone, just near my dirty boot. There is a tall, dark shape standing over us. I look up, and into the face of something awful. I'm so scared that everything seems to pixelate, like reality is disintegrating. But this is all too real.

She has a wide, spiny tooth-filled mouth, teeth and lips limned in dark ichor. Her lips peel back all the way to her stringy black hair, bound by a mask, made of a deer's skull. She wears it like a crown, on the top of her head. The bone is old, one of the antlers snapped off. She growls, low clicking in her throat as she leans over me, cocking her head to the side. She has no nose—just slits. Black, oily eyes with no pupils, stare at me. They're so dangerous, they're almost beautiful.

Her dress is ancient, dirty. Hanging off her in tatters. Once, it may have been beautiful, but now it's just a filmy, gray, off-the shoulder garment that looks like a shroud that's been used. It drags on the floor, hissing. It covers her feet, which pad slowly, bare of any shoes.

Stacia and I lay on the ground, looking up at her helplessly. I could feel her—trying to read my thoughts. She's seeing herself through my eyes. She's awful. Thin. Her spindly fingers reach out, almost touching my face. In the dim glow, they're blackened. She leans forward, her fingers feeling the air above me. She turns towards Stacia.

Of course, I think. Stacia, always the special one. Which means I'm the one who will have to act. I look around, finding that we're surrounded by those small, pale frog-fleshed people. Their eyes are oily, black.

There's a black table, surrounded by warm light, similar to that of the fairy lights I've seen, whenever the Fae have been about. They are not what I thought they were. Tricks, designed to make us relax our guard, let them in. My heart is pounding. I see a wicked-looking sword on the wall behind the table. It is black with age, though the blade is sharp. The hilt is wrapped with darkened twine, a dark gem set into it. It looks like one mentioned in *The Oak Mage*—made of iron, to kill the Fae.

Hope dawns within me. Moving quickly, I raise my hand. Small fingers press down on my shoulders, my head, keeping me where I am. Forcing me to my knees.

She—whatever she is—leans in, gesturing with her spindly-fingered hand. Stacia is pulled to her feet, then brought to the black stone table.

"No!" Stacia screams. Tears track pale paths through the dirt on her face. She is pushed down on the table, held there by two of them. I realize with a sickening lurch the table is not black—it's covered in blood. It smudges my friend's cheek. I can see the whites of Stacia's eyes. Stacia unsheathes the hunting knife she carries, and for a split second, I dare to hope.

"Stacia!" I scream as it is knocked from her grip, clattering on the cave floor. I can't look away. Stacia is staring at me, even as they raise their blade. I watch as all hope leaves her eyes.

"Olive!" she yells. Then the sword falls, my friend's head severing from her neck. I scream, wordlessly. Pain, in my chest, as our bond is severed forever.

CHAPTER TWENTY-EIGHT

2024

REACHING OUT, I GRAB HARLEY'S HAND, he squeezes back. My pulse is racing. His hand is an anchor, keeping me from running the other way.

"Don't let those fuckers grab us," he says. In the light from our head lamps, he holds up his gun. I raise mine, too.

As soon as they enter the light, they stop, jumping back and screaming. I breathe out. "It hurts them—the light."

"Good." He raises his gun and fires. The sound of the shot is immense in the cave.

Inhumanly, they scream, gnashing their teeth. Even in the light, I can't get a good look at them—they're all standing just outside of it. Harley and I both advance. They begin to run, back downward. We sprint to keep up. I grip my gun in shaky hands. We go down, further, further into the ground, the small, hooded figures just outside of the light.

I wish I could use the gun, but I can't figure out how to take the safety off. Beside me, Harley is shooting, causing the cavern to light up. He yells, and I see that several of the Fae have jumped onto him. Harley gets off one more shot, then suddenly I hear him sob. He falls to his knees, drops his guns.

"I—I can't," he says, like an epiphany. "I can't hurt them, Olive." Panicking, I fumble with my weapon. Something grabs hold of my gun, just as I get the safety off. My lamp lights up the creature's face for a second—dark eyes, long teeth in a cold face.

As our eyes meet, I suddenly feel fuzzy. Everything suddenly stills, goes very distant. Almost like I'm in a dream, floating under very deep water.

Let it go. The voice is clear, like a bell. My fingers let go of the gun. It drops to the floor with a clatter. The creature vanishes into the darkness, and I am suddenly released. What just happened?

I scrabble to find it, not letting the creatures out of my field of vision. I breathe a sigh of relief when my hand clamps down on gunmetal. I look all around me. They're just a seething, screaming, clicking mass of creatures.

"I let go. I just…let go," Harley mumbles, pressing his back to mine. I can feel him, shaking.

"Me too." Though, that's not the actual problem. I don't think I can shoot them, though I don't know why. I'm compelled to not do anything. I can only hope I won't regret it later.

In the lull, they seem to multiply around us.

I'm grabbed from behind—small cold fingers, wrapping around my arms. Something child-sized jumps onto my back, knocks off my head lamp. I can hear it breaking, then darkness. There is scrabbling in the dark. Harley cries out suddenly, and then, his light goes out too.

We are brought onward, small hands pushing us forward. I knew it would come to this again: traveling downward into the darkness, against my will. My boots make crunching sounds in the gravel. There is the familiar soft glow in the dark, when I look down, the floor is covered in bones. When I lift my foot, I see teeth scattered about. I glance up, and into the face of the Fae Queen. She lifts her mask to show her true face. Her teeth are red in this lighting, and she leans in towards me. Her dirty dress drags in the dirt, causing the bones on the floor to rattle. Her cold fingers caress my face, her long nails trailing gently over my skin. I can see how I mistook her for Stacia. She imitates, she consumes. I look at the pile of skulls by the table. Children's skulls, their dark eye sockets stare blankly back at me. I wonder which is Stacia. My best friend has been here, the whole time. Dahlia too. There's one that's recent, but the blood is dried. A week, maybe more. None are more recent—none are adult. Dad and Ada are still alive. I blink back tears as I face her. The Queen.

She's been waiting for me, all these years. Still wearing her shroud and broken deer skull. She's gloating, joy coming off her in waves. She makes an odd clicking sound, in the depths of her throat. It reminds of the sound a pigeon makes.

"Where's my father?" I demand.

She hisses. She understands me. Perhaps, she just can't form the words. She leans in, running her fingers along my cheek. Almost tenderly. My flesh rises in goosebumps at her familiar touch.

"Where is he?" I repeat.

She turns away. When I look up, I see they're pressing Harley to the table, just like they did Stacia. My stomach free falls. They're hungry.

"Let him go," I beg. "Let him go."

"Olive," he yells, the whites of his eyes bared as he stares up at the knife.

"No," I scream as the knife makes its downward arc. Harley's scream is cut short. Hot drops of blood spatter my face. I watch in horror as the Fae scoop up handfuls of his blood, drinking it like it's the finest wine. In that moment, I know that unless I'm smart, that's going to be my fate. I fall heavily on my knees and vomit.

WHEN I'm done, I wipe my mouth. What is left of Harley has been swarmed. In the blood-light, his lifeblood is black. They are all drinking it, licking it from his skin. Something tosses his head, and it lands on the ground with a sick thump. I can't believe he's gone. His eyes stare at me, empty. Tears are streaming down my face as I breathe heavily. I'm leaning on my hands, the gravel cutting my palms. Not gravel, I realize. Broken, gnawed bones, teeth. The sweet smell of death is all around me.

In my mind, Harley says, "Get moving. Get out of here. There's nothing you can do." My limbs are locked. Not two feet from where I'm kneeling, there is a skull staring back at me. Dark hair still stuck to its head. The skeleton beside the skull is wearing her clothes. I know that I'm looking into Stacia's eyes.

A hot tear slips down my cheek. I have missed my friend, assuming that she's been alive this whole time. But she hasn't. Time stopped for her twenty-four years ago.

The Queen and her minions are consuming the body. Her hands are wet with Stacia's blood. No, this time, it's Harley's. Fuck. History is repeating. It repeats over and over again, when humans make the mistake of trusting the Fae. Of underestimating them.

How did I get out of this the last time? I wonder.

You made a deal, a husky female voice says in my head. The Fae Queen turns to me, her dirty, bloody dress making a hissing noise in the dust as she walks to me. She leans in, her warm, wet fingers brushing my cheek. *I have the father. I knew if I took him, then you would come back to me. Especially when the form of the girl didn't work.*

She has been posing as Stacia, taking the form of someone that I would let my guard down with. She's been luring me here, hoping I would still follow Stacia into the very depths of Hell. She was, in a way, correct.

He's alive? I don't dare hope. Not yet. She's fooled me before.

Very much so.

I have a sinking feeling. *What do you want?*

I see pictures, in my mind, as she runs her bloody fingers through my hair. It's me, but recently. Sleeping in my childhood bed. I wake, then come running to the window. The words, *Welcome Home, Olive* written backwards in the condensation on the glass with her long finger.

Me, standing in the woods, calling out. Me, standing in my apartment, dropping my glass of wine. Then, earlier. Me and Stacia in the woods. Dancing, with flower crowns on our heads.

She's been watching me. She has always been watching me.

Then I see my mother, standing in the woods. She looks so young. I realize she's younger than I am now.

Please, she calls out, setting down a bouquet of flowers. *I want a daughter.* She's not the first to come to ask this of the Queen. Nor is she the last. My mother, staggering to the stone table, putting her head down. No one is forcing her, I note. She looks into the Queen's eyes. *Keep my daughter safe, please don't hurt her.* The Queen kept her promise. My mother died to keep me from coming here. Tears are streaming down my cheeks. She was protecting me.

Then, my father, walking into the caves. He holds out something. It's wrapped. She takes it, unwraps it. Annabelle Parker's diary, though there's something off about it—the cover is new, I realize. He switched it with the real diary.

It was my duty, I suddenly remember. To bring her the diary. The one book which holds her secrets. I wonder where my father put the real one.

You are mine, Fae Queen tells me, her long fingers running through my hair. *You have always been mine. Since he brought me what I sent you for, I will let your father go, but only if you stay.*

Why?

I can feel it—an overwhelming feeling of emptiness. Darkness. She is my opposite. I can see how she hungers for the light within me. It was never Stacia she wanted. It was me. She wants *me* back.

"Let my father go," I tell her. "Let me take him back. Let me take Ada back."

In exchange?

"I will return to you." I have twelve years, right? My mind is racing. There's still so much I want to do. I want to return to Mila. Make things right between us. Say goodbye.

No. I've waited long enough. You come now.

Very well. Now. I say it, in her language.

It is done.

CHAPTER TWENTY-NINE

2024

SMALL HANDS GRIP ME, LEAD ME OUT. They are gentle this time. I remember leaving this way, many years ago. Because of my mother's sacrifice, I was returned to my father. We were wrong. We were all wrong, about everything. My eyes smart in the light of the sun. I run out of the cave, to find my father. He's unconscious, lying on the ground.

"Dad? Daddy?" I kneel beside him. He's dirty, his gray t-shirt and jeans are torn. His eyes crack open, blinking in the sudden sunlight. It's a miracle. I can't think why my father would be spared, but Harley wasn't. It's beyond me. I'm just grateful one of us will walk out of here.

He groans. "Olive? You came?" His eyes are wide, surprised. He didn't think I'd come, which stings.

He sits up and I wrap my arms around him as tears stream down my cheeks. "I was so worried that you were dead," I reply. "Of course, I came." It's as close as we're going to get to a reunion.

"I thought I was a goner, myself. It was always dark. I couldn't see them." He's blinking muzzily. There's more gray in his hair, I note, than the last time that I saw him.

"We were wrong," I tell him. "Mom didn't leave us."

His face crumples. "No. I figured it out. I found her letter to you that you left in your drawer. I opened it and read it."

As we're talking, there are footsteps. We turn to find that Ada is walking out. Her eyes are wide, frightened. She's pale and dirty, but unharmed, I note with relief.

"Where's Mommy?" she asks.

"Come on, we'll take you to her," I say, reaching out for her hand. She takes it, her fingers cold. We get up and begin walking.

"I knew that if I brought her the diary, she would let me go. She did." He's crying, tears running down his cheeks. "She was angry, about the exhibit I did, but I knew that what she was after was you, the diary."

"Where's Mom's letter?" I ask. He pulls it out of his pocket, hands it to me. It's yellowed, crumpled. I hold it. Herein lies the answers that I need. I put it into my pocket. I'll read it as soon as I'm alone. We walk in silence. My father has stopped crying. Ada clings to my hand.

As we pass the creek, I glance at it, but I don't see the kelpie. Everything seems normal. The sun glinting off the water, the darting shapes of the fish. The woods are silent, except for the wind rustling through the leaves, the water flowing. I feel like I've been emptied out. I avoid thinking of Harley. There's a sharp pain that accompanies that thought.

(his eyes)

(OLIVE!)

If I do, I won't make it through the rest of what I need to do to finish what we started. Finally, we're standing at the edge of the woods. I stop walking. Dad and Ada walk a few steps, until they realize I've stopped. Dad looks at me, frowning.

"I have to go back," I tell him. I know he must have thought this would be a new beginning—that we would be able to start over again. But it's not. This is the end. What could have been will never be.

"No, Olive," he says.

"I promised her."

"Olive! Why would you?"

"Because I wanted to save you." The tears are falling down my cheeks. "She's not going to kill me. She just wants to keep me with her."

"You can't go back," he says. Ada watches, silently. I've let go of her hand.

"If I don't, then you'll never be safe. You're the only one with all the proof, Dad. She'll never let you live, unless she has what she wants, and she knows you gave her a fake version of Annabelle's diary." I need to lie to him now, to get him to go. "And maybe someday, I'll be able to free myself. But you've got to let me go now."

For a long moment, he pauses. Then, finally, he nods, then hugs me. He's thinner than I remember. The light within me tells me all I need to know: cancer is eating him through. He'll be dead by next winter. I will never see him again.

"I know that you're stronger than her," he says, leaning to whisper in my ear: "Go to the cabin." I smile and nod sadly. I watch as he takes Ada's hand and leads her out of the woods.

I know I'm her equal. But I also know that humans will never be able to penetrate her dark fortress beneath the Earth. I have to leave him with some sort of hope, even if it's a lie. I watch him as he stumbles out of the forest. He looks back only once.

Ada does, too, her oily black eyes blink at me. I gasp, realizing that I don't have all of the answers—not yet, at least. Ada grins, baring her spindly teeth, and then turns back around. She's not human. She has never been.

CHAPTER THIRTY

2024

DEAREST OLIVE,

You were my fairy tale ending. My happily ever after. Now, the Queen wants her price. I cannot bring you back. Not at all. I couldn't live with my own broken heart, and your father's, too. So, I'm going in your stead. I hope that you can forgive me, some day.

I asked them for a daughter, there at the black well. When you came along, I knew that it was meant to be, and that I would do anything for you.

As I enter Annabelle's cabin, I can feel her, lurking in the shadows. I step towards the mirror, then reach into my pocket and take out the hag stone. Slowly, my heart racing, I hold it up to my eye and peer through it for the first time. I should have known this from the first.

It's like I'm wearing an ill-fitting skin suit. I can see the dark ragged stitches, holding it together. The oily, black wells of my eyes peer out from the holes. At the nose and mouth, there are gaps, baring pale green skin. Hunks of straw hair, stained red, stick out from the head.

My nightmare—it was a memory. It's like *The Silence of the Lambs*; I'm Hannibal Lecter, wearing someone else's face over my own. I bare my teeth—they're spiny; my slender tongue dances over their points. Why don't I remember who—what I really am? How long have I been pretending to be human?

True horror fills me as the final puzzle piece clicks into place. I remember Stacia, smiling and laughing when she looked at me through the hag stone. She knew. The whole time, she knew what I was. And was still my friend.

Mom didn't know, I realize, thinking of the woman who sacrificed herself for me. She didn't know what I've now come to realize. And that's this: I belong with the folk who live in the woods. Because I am one of them.

The woman who was my surrogate mother died for love. She died to protect a lie. I let the letter in my hand fall to the ground, then I drop the hag stone, too. This is the destruction that the Queen who lives in the woods has wrought. I think about all the mothers—starting with Annabelle—who she has destroyed over the years with her changelings. How many? How many of us are there?

I realize I became a mortician because I was looking for something—another changeling, wrapped in false skin. I hear a rustling by the door, and I turn towards the small, hooded figure slowly. Holding out her hand, she offers me dark, jewel-like seeds. I reach out my hand, taking them and slipping them into my mouth. They taste like late autumn sunlight and woodsmoke.

Peering into the mirror through the stone again, I see a loose thread, hanging down over my forehead. I tug. It's like tearing out a hangnail, that same keen pain. Slowly, the stitches begin to come undone. Gritting my teeth, I keep pulling the thread loose, and the skin opens. Slipping my fingers into the seam, I break myself open like a chrysalis, shedding the skin suit I've worn for three decades. It hurts. My dull human teeth fall out with a clatter on the floor. Slowly, painfully, I ease my skin off. I gasp as it tears away and the soft chartreuse of my true flesh is revealed. I let it fall to the ground as I am reborn.

Memory returns. Long memory, that is darker and deeper than time itself. I remember the promise I made when I was given to Isabelle Sanderson, the daughter she wished for. Then, farther back, to another surrogate mother: Annabelle Parker.

HOLLOW GIRLS

Me, Ada, even Jackie Morton—we're all hollow girls. Monsters in the guise of children. Twelve years later, we return to the Deeping Woods, to our people, to our Queen. Changelings, all of us. A part of a cycle, one which brings real children into the caves. Fresh blood to feed our people.

I have spent centuries looking for genuine love, kindness. And I have found it, among humans. Yet I am bound to her in a way that I cannot break. I am immortal, in ways that humans would never understand. My soul is empty like a benediction, only words echoing like the caves we were banished to.

I turn to my other mother's ghost. I watch as the decomposing of her skin unbecomes. Her face is as I knew it, her eyes so blue, hair auburn. She holds out her hand, cupping my cheek. She fades away, forever. She has finally seen me come home. *Viola*, she whispers, my name hanging on the air.

Turning to the hearth, I take the locket with our pictures, slipping the silver chain over my head. Then, I leave, walking into the woods. As I walk through the trees, they are all lit up with secret signs. I kneel in front of a rock. It's completely ordinary to the human eye. With my Fae eyes, it glows. I reach out and the door swings open.

When I enter the cave, it's no longer dark. I can see all around me, with eyes like their own. They are more beautiful than humans, with eyes that burn like fire. I am surrounded by small figures, chittering. In a moment, it begins to register—a language I have long forgotten. These are my people. I belong here with them.

I see the Queen, waiting in the distance. She's a hulking, ugly figure. She's pleased with my return. I can feel her, wanting me. Usually, it's a homecoming. This time, though, something is different. I know more than I ever have. The faces of all the humans who have loved me and died for me are all in my mind, and a deep, dark anger glows within me, makes me watchful for my moment, my revenge.

Made in the USA
Middletown, DE
04 April 2024